Mary M. Shedd

Gertrude Mason!

Mary M. Shedd

Gertrude Mason!

ISBN/EAN: 9783337318833

Printed in Europe, USA, Canada, Australia, Japan

Cover: Foto ©Andreas Hilbeck / pixelio.de

More available books at **www.hansebooks.com**

A DRAMA

– IN –

FOUR ACTS.

—o—

CHARACTERS:

JAMES HILTON - - -	A Wealthy Banker of Glendale.
CHARLES VAUGHN - -	Collegiate and Banker of Banchester.
ERNEST VAUGHN - - -	Son of Charles Vaughn.
HARRY HANFORD - - -	Young Lawyer of Glendale.
HOFIUS THADDEUS HASKINS -	Country Nephew of James Hilton.
HESTHER HOWARD - - -	House-Keeper.
HAROLD WATSON - -	Brother-in-law of Mrs. Howard.
LOCENO DILUPPA - -	Italian Music Teacher.
MABEL HILTON - - -	Daughter of James Hilton.
GERTRUDE MASON - -	Orphan Niece of James Hilton.
MINNIE WATSON - - -	Daughter of Harold Watson.
SUE WRIGHT - - - -	Hofins' Sweet-heart.
NORA McCARTY - - - -	Servant.
TIM FINNEGAN - - -	Nora's Lover.

—o—

BUCHANAN, MICH.
"INDEPENDENT" BOOK AND JOB ROOMS.
1883.

Gertrude Mason,

ACT I. SCENE I.

Parlor elegantly furnished—two chairs: Enter Hilton from left, Vaughn following.

HILTON:—*(from out-side)* "Come in James; this is an unexpected pleasure; be seated." *(both sit; Vaughn at right.)* "It has been a long time since I saw you; not since I was at Banchester, three years ago."

VAUGHN:—' Yes, I really believe it has been three years.'

HILTON:—"We grow old so rapidly, it would be better to see each other occasionally, that we may not forget."

VAUGHN:—"I think it is out of the question for you and I to forget each other; but to tell you the truth James, you are getting to be so old and homely, it is more disagreeable to look at you, than you may think."

HILTON:—"I acknowledge it now; but when we were young and at college together, you where in the shade. But I am not going to quarrel with you if you are a little better looking now, as it never troubled you when I was at the head."

VAUGHN:—"Why do you think it did not trouble me? I have thought seriously of murdering you at several different times, but I am thankful that I did not; for now I have the sweet satisfaction of being best looking."

HILTON:—"I acknowledge it. Say, by the way, did your son, Ernest, accompany you to the city?"

VAUGHN:—"No, he is coming this week."

HILTON:—"Ernest is still unmarried I presume?"

and we sincerely hope you will care for each other. (*Mabel starts*) Ernest is a model young man, very much like his father; thoughtful, kind to the poor and the uniting of your fortunes would place both independent for life. By doing this, Mabel, you would confer a life-long blessing upon us and I feel as though it could not be otherwise."

MABEL:—Why Papa—supposing we were not agreeable to each other, would you have us marry contrary to our wishes?

HILTON:—" Certainly not, my dear, if it could be prevented; but Mabel, you were raised in luxury and to live without it life would be a burden. You know nothing of want, therefore, if love or wealth must be omitted, love should be the sacrifice."

MABEL:—" Judging the future from the past, I do not think there will be much love sacrificed on my part. Oh! dear, I did not want to marry any one; but then, Papa, if you really wish it I will do so to please you, for it is nothing to me particularly. But Ernest may object? At least, I should think he would if he is a sensible young man."

HILTON:—" Mabel, I want you to think of it seriously, and do try to be a little more dignified; you lost a great deal of your dignity in your visit to the country last summer. I do not object to your nonsense my dear, but Ernest is refined and elegant, and it may displease him. By pleasing him you please your father."

MABEL:—" I know I'll not please him, I know it! I never possessed any amount of dignity, but my visit in the country gave less, and more of real life. Papa, they did not live in luxury, and there life was not a burden."

HILTON:—" A few weeks of such a life are enjoyable, but for a live time, it would be misery to you. (*Goes to her, puts his hand on her head.*) Do not think I want to scold you, my little pet, but try to be a little more earnest in manners—a little more dignity, that's all.

MABEL:—" I presume I will do something wrong, awfully stupid. (*rises.*) I know he will dislike me; I know he cannot ever care so much for me as you do. If I must marry him, I want to stay here. I could not leave you, Papa, to go with any one."

HILTON:—" Do not be foolish darling, you will feel differently. Mabel, when I married your mother, I cared more for her, and she for me, than it is possible for a child to care for a parent. You will some day know the strength of love."

MABEL:—" Then, Papa you did not marry for mere fortune, did you?"

HILTON:—" No! No! but people nowadays must have wealth. What could you do with out it? Think of it, Mabel, and try to feel as I do. But I must arrange my papers, for Ernest may be here any moment." (*Exit, left.*)

MABEL:—" Now! don't that beat all? Why that is the very last thing I should have thought of doing. Getting married! falling in love! dead earnest, as cousin Hofius says. Falling in love and getting married or, getting married then fall in love. Ha! ha! but I would not do that—no sir! if I can't fall in love, and awfully, too, why I shall not marry, and Papa would never compel me to do it, either. He would never compel me to do anything I disliked, I always have my own way. Yes, I suppose papa would be happy if Ernest and I should fall in love, first sight, Ernest propose, I accept, get married and go to keeping house, and he come visiting. Of course, it is all right, but I feel as though I was being peddled for—oh, mercy, mercy! There are words that would be appropriate to my feelings, and if I was down in the country with Cousin Hofius I'd spit 'em out, too; but Papa says I must be more dignified. He his determined to have me take Ernest, perhaps I had better. Yet, I cannot help thinking what a difference there is between Papa and I in the selection of a husband. The one I would select would be compelled to exercise brain and muscle to get his living; a good character, good looking, not a cent of his own, poor and proud. But I presume Papa thinks I couldn't work, but I know better. I would like to work as Cousin Grace did, down in the country; great dish apron on, sleeves rolled up to her chin, hands splashing in the dish water, clearing off the table, gathering up the crumbs for the chickens, cows, pigs and horses. I know I would make a good farmer's wife. Yes, I would do all that for some poor fellow's sake; presume I shall never have the pleasure of choosing for myself; seems as though everything disagreeable is happening at once. Mrs. Howard tries to make Papa think that she has been accustomed to elegance and is now obliged to depend, principally, on her labor, and Papa is always so good to the poor, he is quite willing to lend a sympathizing ear, and she trying to make love to Papa!"

(*Bell rings, enter Nora, left.*)

NORA:—" A gentleman to see your father,"

MABEL:—(*looking at card*) Ernest Vaughn, my future husband, I suppose. Here, Nora, give this to Papa and show the gentleman into the library."

NORA:—"Say, say, Miss Mabel, is this your intended for sure?"

MABEL:—"No! no! Nora; you may dust the room when you return. (*exit Nora.*) I wonder if Ernest is going to feel as silly as I do! he! he! he! *I* feel silly enough and presume I will act accordingly. Well, now I must be womanly, dignified, grand and glorious, to please Papa and Ernest. I suppose Papa wonders why I do not come in the library. I may as well start, so here goes to fall in love!" [*Exit.*] *Enter Nora at left.*

NORA:—(*dusting*)" Well, I niver seed the loike of Miss Mabel snapping me up in that way! I tell yis it wouldn't be Nora McCarty that would be ashamed of sich an illegant chap as that. No, no, ha! ha! I'd not be ashamed of that young gintleman, not me. [*laughing*] (*Enter Mrs. Howard.*) Ah! goodness mercy! yis almost scared the sinses out of me."

HOWARD:— (*sternly*) " Nora, who is in Mr. Hilton's library?"

NORA:—"A young gintleman. I'll tell yis, Mrs. Howard, but plase keep still about it; I raley belave it is Miss Mabel's intended husband. Now don't you brathe it for the world, but I raley, raley belave it is her swate-heart. Ah! he is a *beautiful* young man!"

HOWARD:—"I only wish it was some one to marry her and take her away from here."

NORA:—"Now that is quare talk! I tell yis, Mrs. Howard, this a better place than you would find if yis were to advertise a month."

HOWARD:—"I hardly think I would advertise! (*While Nora is dusting Mrs. Howard steps to one side and talks to herself*) Yes, indeed, I wish she would marry, then I would be sure of winning Mr. Hilton. He has sympathy for the poor, but that daughter, Mabel,—how I hate her! To be her servant is more than my proud nature can endure; yet he shall never know how I feel toward her." (*Enter Hofius at left. Nora and Mrs. H. look astonished.*)

HOFIUS:—"Good day! I come round to the side door and found it unlocked so, I didn't stop to knock or ask any questions. Is Mabel about? Mr. Hilton lives here, don't he."

HOWARD;—(*sternly*) " Why, sir, you must be a very intimate friend!"

HOFIUS:—" Well, should rather say I was. His sister was

my mother; he is my uncle and Mabel is my cousin, my first cousin, too. Darn it! I'd like to see her, but if she is busy I can wait. (*takes seat, Nora stands staring.*) Plenty things to look at while I'm waiting."

HOWARD;—" Then you are a relative, are you?"

HOFIUS:—" Course I am. Why, didn't you ever hear Mabel speak of her Cousin Hofius Thaddeus Haskins what lives down at Squash Holler on the Mud Creek division? Yes, I am her cousin, first cousin, too, and between you and me, I think a darn sight of her."

HOWARD:—" Were the family expecting you?"

HOFIUS:—" I wrote to them, last winter, something about coming up here to study Elocution, so I guess they wont be much surprised to see me. Say! (*to Nora*) if you are the hired girl just step round and tell Mabel, or ask her if she wouldn't be glad to see her Cousin Hofius? I bet, ha! ha! she will scamper in here quicker than you can say Jack Robinson. Now see if she don't. (*Nora remains still looking at him.*) Well, stand there if you don't care about going, I enjoy looking round tolerable well. (*exit Nora L.*) Now these walls are a darned sight higher than the room is wide. (*to Mrs. H.*) What did you say your name was?"

HOWARD:—" I do not remember of telling my name, but if you are a nephew of Mr. Hilton's I would as soon tell you; it is Mrs. Howard."

HOFIUS:—" Why you needn't have told me 'till you got ready, I didn't care particularly; but then you know when a fellow is among strangers he must say something to keep the conversation going; then, folks from the country don't go much on brass."

HOWARD: "No? You must excuse me as your cousin will soon be in." [*Exit*] *Enter Mabel.*

MABEL:—" Why, Coz., you old darling, when did you arrive?" (*Hofius shakes both hands.*

HOFIUS:—" Oh! come about an hour ago. I had the blastedest time getting here! I took the wrong car and didn't find it out till I had paid my five cents. Some darn city upstart said I had better have a label pinned on my hat. For tew cents I'd have pinned a black spot over his eye."

MABEL:—" Sit down. Coz. I came very near going down to your home again this summer, but could not. I am glad you are here. But did we not enjoy gathering apples and riding on the great wagons of hay? I never had so much fun in my life!"

HOFIUS:—" Fun? fun is no where! I was lonesome enough to die after you came home, and I never sild down them old straw stacks once without thinking of you."

MABEL:—" Ha! ha! O dear! I did enjoy myself, but Hof., if you should tell Papa that I did such rediculous things, he would be terribly shocked. Don't ever expose me. (*Bell rings, enter Nora with letter which she hands to Mabel. She looks at Hofius suspiciously.*)

NORA :—" A letter for you, Miss Mabel." (*Mabel takes letter and opens it.*)

MABEL:—" It is from Cousin Gertie; I hope she is coming. I will read it. (*reads*) 'DEAR MABEL: At last I find myself free from school, free from any duties that bind me here; therefore, I accept your kind invitation.' Yes she is coming!

HOFIUS:—" Well, I never seen her, but if you are glad I am, too."

MABEL:—" Yes, you must be glad, she is so nice; but I must finish my letter; (*reads*) 'Three years ago to-day my mother died; the loneiness of those years are known only to an orphan. No father to care for me, no mother to love me; dear Mabel, is life worth living? I am so lonely I long to be with you, as you and uncle are the only ones that seem to care for me. I shall be with you soon—to-morrow, perhaps. Until then, good bye;
Your Affectionate Cousin,
GERTIE.

HOFIUS:—" I'll bet she is a boss girl, but that letter makes a feller feel kindy sober, don't it? Where does she live, any way?"

MABEL:—" Here comes Papa and Mr. Vaughn. I must not smile again." (*Enter Hilton, Ernest following L. H.*)

HILTON:—" Hofius, I am glad to see you! (*shakes hands and introduces Ernest*) Mr. Vaughn, my nephew, Mr. Haskins." *Ernest bows, Hofius moves toward him shakes, hands.*

HOFIUS:—" I am glad to know you sir, but I didn't understand the name?" (*still holding Ernest's hand.*)

ERNEST:—" Vaughn is my name!"

HOFIUS:—A-ha! (*releases hand*) why there used to be a family down in Squash Holler by that name; (*raises voice*) they stole all my father's chickens the last year they were there, and bothered the geese most to death; break their legs and pull out their wing feathers. But they moved away a long time ago. Don't suppose they were any relation of yourn? but then the boys must be grown up by this time. You never lived near Squash Holler, did you?"

ERNEST:—"No, I do not know that I ever heard of the place."

HOFIUS:—"Well, you don't look much like the Squash Holler chaps. You see, 'taint a very big town but we have a heap of fun down there, don't we, Mabel?"

MABEL:—"Yes, indeed."

HOFIUS:—"Don't you remember we had fun (*Mabel scowls at him*) when we had so many nice buggy rides? You haven't told your father about getting that letter."

MABEL:—"No, I haven't. Papa, I received a letter from Cousin Gertie, she will be here soon."

HILTON:—"That will be pleasant for all of you, as she is a very interesting young lady; her school is finished, is it not?"

ERNEST:—(*To Mabel*) "Your cousin, did you say?"

MABEL:—"Yes, sir; a young lady from Sand Hill."

ERNEST:—"The little hamlet we find only by means of stage?"

MABEL:—"The same, sir. She will help to make your visit pleasant as she sings very prettily, but is rather timid."

ERNEST:—"I presume I shall enjoy her society, but really, I never fancied country innocense as much as a great many."

MABEL:—"Yot may feel differently; for, with all her simplicity of manner, she possesses an uncommon amount of good sense, ever aspiring to fathom what others would call a mistery and let it pass. Enjoys music and plays nicely. We have the same teacher, Loceno Diluppa, and he is very loud in his praise of her voice, and I think she will resume her music with me when she arrives." (*Bell rings.*)

HILTON:— (*Rising*) "There is the bell for lunch; come Ernest and Hofius, we will have some refreshments." (*Exit Hilton L.*)

HOFIUS:—"All right. I tell you I feel gant enough."

MABEL:—"I must arrange this music as Loceno will be here and I want him to examine it before I take my lesson." (*arranges music then follows; enter Nora R.*)

NORA :— (*brushing hurridly*) " I tell yis I must fly around.
I have two dozen things to do this very minnit. That cousin
of Miss Mabel's is a quare looking chap. I thought I'd laugh
the life out o' me to see the figger he makes. Ha! he! he! he
looks the most like Tim of any body I've put me eyes on since
I left ould Oireland. I do wonder if the young lady that
is to be here soon is the curiosity that this gintleman is! If
she is we will have some of Barnum's foinest specimens. Um
um, yis, yis, ha! ha! that cravat is about as short as the coat."

Enter Loceno, L. with guitar and music.

LOCENO :—(*sets guitar in corner.*) I shall remain here until
Mabel calls for me. Has Gertie arrived?"

NORA :—" No, sir; nobody has arrived but a young gintleman." (*Exit L.*)

LOCENO :—" A gentleman! a young gentleman! If he dares
to come between Gertie and I he shall suffer. Ah, Gertrude
Mason! you do not love me as I do you; but I saved your
mother's life and she gave you to me. Yes, you have promised
to marry me, (*walking around room*) and your money is not
objectionable. I know, little Gertie, you do not love me as I
do you, not enough to marry me, but you think a promise
sacred as life, and you shall be made to keep it." (*enter Nora L.*)

NORA :—" Please sir, Miss Mabel is a waiting for yis in the
sitting room." (*Exit Nora, Loceno following with guitar and
music. Enter Hilton with paper, Ernest following.*

HILTON :—" Ernest, please be seated. You will excuse me
for half an hour or so. Here is the paper till I can join you, or
Mabel will be in presently. I will return soon as possible."

ERNEST :—" I can amuse myself with the paper, thanks.
(*Exit Hilton at left.*) I do not care for the paper, I have
enough to think of at present without reading. So this Miss
Mabel is the young lady my father wishes me to wed! I know
I am my fathers idol, and I thought I could never refuse to
comply with any request he might make; but I fear this is too
much. She is far from pleasing to me, and I am twice as disagreeable to her. I only hope we may feel differently, as
pleasing my father is my greatest joy. (*Enter Nora at right.
Two expressman follow with trunk; she stands aside; they pass
her.*

NORA :—" Mr. 'Spressman, go straight ahead, through that
door, (*pointing at left entrance*) turn at the right, go straight
ahead through the hall, up that first flight of stairs, pass along
to next door. (*follows them out into the hall and is heard talk-*

ing without.) That isn't the door, but the next door right across the hall; that door is the door, down wid the trunk! (*set down trunk*) Now come back the same way yis went. *Nora appears, they pass by her and out, when Ernest speaks to her.*

ERNEST:—" Nora, whose trunk is that ?"

NORA :—" It is the property of Miss Mabel's cousin, Gertrude Mason. Ah! she is a swate gairl; very innocent gairl and its very pretty, too, ye'll find her."

ERNEST: —" I do not doubt it. I presume she is very innocent, child-like and bland!" (*Sneeringly.*)

NORA :—" Yis, your right. She is as innocent as the day is long." *Exit L.*

ERNEST:—(*sneeringly*) " I shall certainly have a delightful time! Unsofisticated innocense! And now I hope Harry will call in to-day, or soon, he would be of some service. One young lady too childish and frivolous for any heart; the other so much heart there can be no character! Nothing in either I so much admire in women. Mabel's only redeeming qualities are her independence and kindness to the poor. I wish Harry was here!" (*Enter Mabel, Gertie leaning on her arm.*)

MABEL:—" Mr. Vaughn, allow me the pleasure of introducing my cousin, Miss Mason." (*Ernest and Gertie bow.*)

ERNEST :—" Miss Mason, I am pleased to meet you."

GERTIE:—(*bowing*) " Thanks. I am glad to know there is another depending on Cousin Mabel's hospitality."

ERNEST:—" Yes; but she is sometimes a little sarcastic, therefore I shall look to you for sympathy." (*Mabel laughs.*)

GERTIE:—" Certainly; the one most deserving my sympathy shall have it."

ERNEST:—" You two are so devoted to each other, I am terribly afraid I shall be slighted, therefore, I warn you to be cautious, as I am prepared to be jealous."

GERTIE:—" I do not believe you will have any cause for jealousy, as we would not slight you."

MABEL:—" Ah! Gertie, that sounds just like your honest self; you would not offend; Ernest is accustomed to having his own way. Now, it would be better for his health to have opposition occasionally. I do not intend to discommode myself beyond reason for the sake of being too agreeable.

ERNEST:—" Even if you were, I have a faint idea the result would be a failure." (*All laugh; enter Loceno, left.*)

LOCENO:—" I do not wish to disturb you, ladies, but do you wish to continue your lessons during Gertrude's visit ?"

MABEL:—" We are to continue; we must learn some new duets."

LOCENO:—" Very well; I hope you will enjoy yourselves. (*Looks at Gertie.*) Remember your promise! (*Exit left; Gertie looks sad.*)

MABEL:—" What can he mean? Why do you look so sad, Gertie? I cannot see your face so gloomy. (*Rises*)) I must show you my flowers; they are beautiful, ar'n't they, Ernest?

ERNEST:—"Yes, very." (*Mabel clenches her hat in mock tragedy.*)

MABEL:—"Me hat! let me clutch thee whilst I fly and prepare the way for those who, perchance, may follow. (*Turns to them.*) "You two are perchance." (*Walks off in march time, exit right; Ernest bows low and offers arm to Gertie, who rises and places hand on arm.*)

ERNEST:—" We must be equal to the occasion, sir; come into the garden, Maud, we'll view the little flowers fair." (*Exit, following Mabel; enter Nora replacing tidies on chairs.*)

NORA:—" Ah! dear, I am nearly wild wid so much work. It's Nora here, it's Nora there, and Nora, Nora, everywhere. Och! That's poecry (*Looks out of the window.*) Ah! there they are, all the young men and girls. I'll tell yez: This love-making is awful swate. The swatest part of your life is in the love-making toime. I remember so well the avenin' I left ould Erin. I stood upon the shore, a'harkin' to tha roar. Ah! shure an' that was another snatch of poecry—why, Nora, what are ye a'comin' to? Nothing veary strange for me; mither always told us children that we were all naturally born to be something; but vil niver open me mouth to her about it. But, as I was standing on the shore a'harkin' to the roar, I looked down at me soide—there was me little parcel, me all. I said to meself, won't Tim come and kiss his swate-neart good-bye? Just that vary second some one tapped me on the shoulder and says: 'Nora, me darlint, must ye lave me? (*sobbing.*) Me heart was throbbing, me eyes full o' tears; (*wipes eyes with apron*) says oi, 'Tim, is it you?' Says Tim, 'Is it you?' Then I smelt his breath, an' I knew it was Tim. (*Sobbing.*) Ah, Tim! don't yis remember whin ye said: 'Nora, me darlint, must ye lave me?' Well, I clasped him in me arms and he clasped me in his arms, and then we stood wid both our arms around each other. Tim kissed me and I kissed Tim ; the many tha' times I couldn't count. Then I stepped on tha ould boat, and soon I was moving away from ould Oirland, and Tim—— Ah, Tim ! I can see yis standing there, (*waves her hands*) waving yer cap and crying ' farewell, Nora, farewell, farewell.' (*Bell rings.*) Ah, blast it! there goes the devlish bell. No use to talk ; Nora McCarthy can niver git the oppertunity to enjoy a little grafe." (*Exit, left ; enter Mrs. Howard, with flowers.*)

MRS. HOWARD:—" What beauties these flowers are. I do believe James Hilton loves me a little, or he would not send me such lovely boquets or delicacies during my sickness. He is so kind!" (*Re-enter Nora and arranges tidies.*) "Who rang the bell, Nora ?"

NORA :—" A young gentleman, Mr. Ernest Vaughn, and I sent him into the garden wid the others, for you know they were all in there together ; so I sint him out there, as I didn't wait him a'hocking around tha house. Mr. Hilton wishes to see you a few minutes in the library, if you please." (*Exit right.*)

SCENE II.

Small Grove Walk—(Enter Hofius, left.)

HOFIUS:—" Well, this seems a little like home, only we can find words all around us there, so we don't mow down every blade of grass that comes up. We let 'er go for the cows to gnaw off. Darn sight a fooling, here, about a little patch of woods, anyway. Now, Mabel says I must get a longer coat, longer coat tails, and long pants, and I'll bet if I had pants longer than these I'd have 'em all mud in less than half an hour. But, if Mabel says git 'em, I'll do it if we have to sell a cow. There's a darn sight of style hanging around this house, any way, but I will act just as though I was good as any of them, until I get my new things. Then when I go back to Squash Holler, I guess Sue Wright's eyes will stick out for once. I don't see much of a chance for me to study elocution among all these parties, croquets, chess and checker, singing, etc., but guess I will go in the grove and see where they are." (*Exit, right.*)

SCENE III.

Grove—Flowers ; (Harry and Mabel seated back ; Gertie and Ernest near front on rustic seat ; Ernest talking devotedly to Gertie.

ERNEST:—" Dear Gertie, why do you let so foolish a promise as thas of Luceno trouble you a moment? You were young and promised under very sorrowful circumstances, and I should not even think of it, unless you care for him."

GERTIE:—" Care for him? Oh! Ernest, I feel for him an aversion more bitter than I ever thought to have for any human being."

ERNEST:—" My heart, heaven knows, pleads for you; but you cannot dream of the horrible power there is for evil about that man if he chooses."

GERTIE:—" I know it, Ernest, I know it; but my mother taught me never to make a promise that I could not fulfill. It was my instruction from a little child; it is instituted in my nature deep as my life, and as sacred."

ᵔ ERNEST:—" If you leave it to me, trust me. I am sure I can arrange it satisfactorily, Will you not, Gertie."

GERTIE:—" What shall I do? Whenever I fight against him I see so plainly my mother's face telling me to keep my promise, as he saved our lives. But, oh! how intensely I hate him And yet, at times, I have felt irresistably impelled toward him, through the promise. Much as I loath him, to free myself from him entirely, seems an insurmountable obstacle." (*Hilton enters back part unobserved and shows displeasure, then retires.*)

ERNEST:—" But, Gertie, if you can trust me, I am sure I can make him know how ridiculous such a promise is. Do not let it trouble you. (*they arise and walk towards Mabel and Harry.*) Harry you and yours follow. We are going to have another game of—(*Harry and Mabel follow them out at right entrance; scene closes in path as before in scene II*)

SCENE IV.

Hofius returns through path.

HOFIUS:—" Well, here I am in the very same place again A feller can't git lost in a grove. I'd give a sixpence to know what that feller means by talking so much to Mabel. I suppose everbody calls Harry Hanford smart, because he can spout law and wear good clothes; but I think he blows a darn sight. Yet Mabel takes it all down. I'd give a dollar if I didn't thihk so much of that girl, but I do and that's the end of it. (*Exit, L. scene same as in scene 1st.*)

SCENE V.—PARLOR &C.

(Mrs. Howard and Loceno seated.)

LOCENO:—" Mrs. Howard, if you will do that you shall be rewarded."

HOWARD :—" I will do anything I can, but remember you must work for me. There is no mistaking Ernest's love for Gertrude, but we must separate them. We must arrange it so you can marry Gertie soon, then Ernest will take Mabel and I will be free from her insults. Mabel knows her father wishes her to marry Ernest and if I can make Mr. Hilton believe Gertie is trying to win Ernest from Mabel, he will turn against her, and I will make her believe it. He already begins to see. If we are cunning we can arrange it, but don't you give up Gertie. I am sure of getting rid of Mabel ; if you can only take Gertrude away from Ernest, then I can take Mr. Hilton." *(Gertie comes part way in, then, as she notices them, turns to retire, when Loceno grasps her arm, brings her abruptly to the centre of the room, looking directly in her face.)*

LOCENO:—" Ah! little beauty, your place is here with me, not with Ernest Vaughn. Don't you belong to me Gertie? *(She appears frightened and does not answer.)* Why do you not answer me?"

GERTIE :—" I cannot answer you, I do not know."

LOCENO:—" Yes you do know. Do you intend to marry me, or Ernest? You know how I love you, you know I saved your life and your mother's, you know how dear you are to me, and you promised you would marry me. Gertrude you must not lie to me. *(patting her face and kissing her.)* Beautiful one, dear as you are to me, I warn you not to lie to me for the punishment of a liar is worse than that of a murderer when the victim is at the mercy of Loceno Diluppa." *(Gertie weeping ; Mabel enters, and Mrs. Howard leaves immediately at back door ; Mabel grasps Loceno's arm.)*

MABEL:—" Loceno Diluppa, what are you saying, what right have you to talk in this manner?"

LOCENO:—" Gertie should listen to me as she—" *(Mabel interrupts.)*

MABEL:—" She is nothing to you,--there's the door coward."

LOCENO:—" But I tell you—" *(Mabel interrupts.)*

MABEL :—" I want you to tell me nothing. There's the door I tell you, and *(Loceno moves towards the door.)* Return when your cuties call you; all we want is your music, now, go! (*Gertie sits crying*; *Loceno exit muttering to himself*, *Mabel carreses Gertie.*) Dear Gertie, you must not cry, do not give up to everything. Dear little cousin, I shall do something desperate if you continue to feel so badly. That old music teacher shall trouble you no more Gertie, if you love me at all, stop crying."

GERTIE:—"I do love you, Mabel, oh! so much, but I feel as though I shoul'l die." (*Enter Ernest hurriedly, with hat in hana.*)

ERNEST:—" I am going now to take those papers to Harry.. I presume Miss Mabel,—(*voice changes.*) Why what is the trouble with Gertie? In tears again? (*he goes to her, puts hand on head.*) It pains me, Gertie, to see you weeping, if there was anything I could do, how gladly would I do it! I think you rather be alone, so I will go."

MABEL:—" Gertie is a little nervous I think, do not remain away long."

ERNEST:—" So long as Gertie is here, it is useless to mention it. Aurevoir!" (*Bows and retires at L.*)

MABEL:—"There is something indifferent in the tone of Ernest's voice. I am afraid he is not as sincere as he might be."

GERTIE:—" Sincere? what mean you, Mabel? Not sincere in his manner to me?"

MABEL:—" I fear not.',

GERTIE:—" Oh, Mabel! for the love of heaven do not say that again. Anything but that." (*sobs.*)

MABEL:—" I am not sure, I only feared he was not."

GERTIE:—" Could he show so decided a preference, and then cast me aside? No, no! I cannot believe it! I will not! He is all I have left. Uncle does not act the same, he no longer loves me; Mrs. Howard hates me; Loceno haunts me day and night. You and Ernest are the only ones that care for me. No, no, Mabel! Ernest could not be so cruel—to win my love. He knows—he cannot help knowing I love him; although I never told him so, he knows. No! No! I would doubt everyone before I would Ernest."

MABEL:—" Gertie, you are not feeling well; I wish Cousin Hof. would come in, or something happen to cheer you up. (*enter Hofius*) When we attend the party at Mrs. Bell's you will feel better, for she has such nice parties."

HOFIUS:—"I tell you, (*to himself*) I will keep still about this, you bet!"

MABEL:—"Cos., where have you been so long? We were afraid you were lost in the city, but you still live, I see."

HOFIUS:—(*slowly*) "Yes."

MABEL:—"What's the matter, Hofius."

HOFIUS:—"Nothing."

MABEL:—"Then why don't you talk? Haven't you seen anything pretty, funny or hateful?"

HOFIUS:—"Yes, a darn sight more than I wish I had."

GERTIE:—"Now Hofius, Mabel and I are feeling so blue tell us something, wont you?"

HOFIUS:—"I haint got anything to tell unless it is something about me, and it wouldn't tickle you to hear how I got fooled, would it?"

MABEL:—"Cos., you are awful cross, cross as a—"

HOFIUS:—"Wet hen, why don't you say? women always say that."

MABEL:—"Well then, "wet hen," only you are crosser. I wish I knew what troubles you."

HOFIUS:—"It is trouble enough, I tell you! I met a man on the street corner, a darn good looking feller, fine clothes and watch and so on. I was standing on the corner looking around, and he came up to me and says he, I have seen you lots of times, when you have been around town, and he often thought he'd like to know me; so Iup like a fool and told him who I was, where I was staying, how long I was going to stay, what I was doing, how much money I had, and about you two girls. He kindy pricked up his ear when I told him about you girls, and said he'd like to see you. (*Mabel laughs a little.*) You needn't laugh, I did tell him. But I told him you was struck after that young lawyer, or that blow Harry, and I told him Gertie was smiling sweeter than lasses on that long legged Ernest. He looked as though he felt awful sorry, so he asked me to go to his home and see his sister, and I went. I knew Sue Wright would be madder than hops if she knew it, but I went. (*Mabel and Gertie laugh.*) Now see here Mabel, if you are going to laugh, I will dry right up and you won't git another word out of me."

MABEL:—"No! no! Hof we will not laugh again."

HOFIUS:—"'Taint nothing to laugh at. Well I went in with the feller to see Hattie, as he called her, and there sot the beautifulist bewitchingest critter you ever sot eyes on. I never see anything like her; the alfiredist prettiest girl that ever trod down grass. She must a had wings pinned back under that little cape, I know she must. Um, oh! dear! don't like to think of it, but if Is'e to be scratched to death by chickens, I couldn't forget her. Now girls, you know I don't fall in love very easy, but oh. Jupiter! anything from a dove to a man, or a rhinocerous, couldn't help feeling they were a gone up goose when she levelled them eyes on 'em.''

GERTIE;—"I don't doubt it, Hofius, but Mabel and I feel a little interested in the brother. Was he so irresistable?''

HOFIUS:—"That brother, eh? He was a mean cuss! when he got me into the house, and dead in love with them eyes, he asked me to give him two twenty dollar bills and one ten for a fifty. So I changed and he said he would get some fruit and bring in. I sat there a looking at her face and sometimes she looked at me, 'till I asked her if he was coming back. She yaw-hawed right out and said; "I guess not " Well, I got up and got. I asked a police if that bill was good; "No," said he, but he tried to find out about it, and when I left him he said he would try and get the fellow, but I guess he wont find him right away. I tell you, girls, I was awful glad I knew the way home.''

MABEL:—"That's too, too bad, cousin.'' (*Smiling.*)

HOFIUS:—"Yes, but you'd like to laugh, wouldn't you? Laugh if you want to! I've had to work like the devil to get my money, and, by gosh, I don't like to loose it. But 'taint all lost. It's worth twenty-five dollars to have that picture girl, Hattie, smile on you. Oh! um, um! I never can forget her. I'd give five dollars for her picture for you to see. I can't forget her, but I shan't tell Sue Wright about her when I go home again. Say, now, don't tell Uncle James about this or he will think I am greener than Mrs. Wright's old bonnet strings. I'll get them new clothes you talked of. I'll get them right off and wear them.''

MABEL:—"I won't tell. I am glad you are going to get your new clothes.''

HOFIUS:—" I am going to commence my elocution lessons, too.''

MABEL:—"Cousin, how did you happen to think of taking elocution lessons?''

HOFIUS:—" Well, I tell you; seeing I have got my hand in to tell all I know, I will keep right on. There was a man, he called himself an elocutionist from Bosting. He came down to Squash Holler and read at the Methodist Church. Well, mother is Methodist, so we all went, paid twenty five cents to git in, and I took Sue Wrights. He read lots of pieces; sometimes he would read things so darned funny, it would make a dog laugh till he'd swaller his ears. Ha! ha! Then he'd read another so sober and so awful solemn (*appears affected*,) our eyes would git chucked full o' tears. I tried to keep back the tears, but I finally bust right out loud. Oh! Mabel, I know you girls would a cried, too. You don't act as though you cared a cent now, but darn ye, I've seen you squall just as loud as anybody."

MABEL:—"I know it Hofius, (*rising*.(I cry awful easy, but I don't feel like crying now. I don't want to and you must not be so cross to me, for you know I like you."

HOFIUS:—"Not so much but what you could git over it if you should see that long toungued pitafogger coming."

MABEL:—"That wouldn't make any difference. Oh! your awful jealous Cos., lets go in the library. What say you Gertie?"

GERTIE:—(*rising.*) "I want to get that new book, so I am ready to go anywhere." (*All go to L. door.*)

HOFIUS:—"So would I be ready to go anywhere if Hattie was to be there. No I can't forget her, I can't." (*Exit.*)

SCENE VI: HARRY'S OFFICE.

Two gentlemen seen writing: Enter Ernest.

ERNEST:—"Friend Hanniford, good morning." (*Harry looks up.*)

HARRY:—"Good morning Ernest."

ERNEST:—"Well, has the morning's rolicking zephyrs brought joy, health and fortune to you, my boy."

HARRY:—"Yes, yes, I'm basking in the sunshine of just such materials as you now mentioned. Come forward, my friend, and be seated and tell us the news."

ERNEST:—"News? oh, Harry! don't be so modest! come out like a man and inquire after Mabel, you know you want to." (*The gentlemen writing take books and leave at back entrance.*)

HARRY:—"I was on the eve of doing so."

ERNEST:—"She is enjoying fine health and wishes to be remembered to you. Do you feel better now?"

HARRY:—"Yes, and I would like to ask for Gertie, yet I fear to do so, as you may get jealous, you know. If you are like me you would. Don't it beat Caesar, that I should be so jealous, so fearfully jealous? Sometimes I think Mabel does not care two cents for me. If I were not so poor in pocket—but I always think of it, always compare my poverty to her wealth. I wish I could think she cared as much for me as Gertie does for you"

ERNEST:—"Gertie, for me? Oh! there is not so much love between us as you imagine; neither of us will go insane over it."

HARRY:—"What do you mean, Ernest, by saying neither of you are particularly interested! If ever I saw a devoted admirer, you are one, or your actions are unaccountable."

ERNEST: "I must play the agreeable, you know, Harry."

HARRY:—"Play the agreeable? In playing the agreeable must you monopolize her entirely for a season, escort her to every party, to picnics, drives and play partner to eve y game? Be constantly with her and show marked attention, always at her elbow? Does it take all of this to be agreeable?"

ERNEST—:"Have I gone through so much? I guess you have told the truth, Harry."

HARRY:—"Of course it's the truth. She has just finished her studies and that Italian teacher is continually harrassing her. No father or mother to care for her, or advise her, she has forgetten all and is happy in your presence. Your unceasing devotion to her has made her feel you cared for her; she is not the kind to love when she is unsought, but you have sought her and now say you care nothing for her. Such things were excusable when you were younger and at college among a crowd of heartless girls; but, Ernest, I was sure you had ceased to indulge in such folly, such heartlessness. I tell you Ernest this is cruel!"

ERNEST:—"I think you are saying a great deal more than is necessary. We have enjoyed each other's society but I could not marry her, she is too wild for me. As I leave here soon I shall take an opportunity to tell her the kind of a woman I should like for a wife, then she will see Harry, how great a difference between herself and my ideal. In that way she will understand I mean nothing serious."

HARRY:—"It is a pretty time to say it now! There are very few men that would put aside so lovely a girl as she. You must remember she has been confined to the school room; but one year abroad in grand society would make her a woman unsurpassed. Besides, Ernest, it is worth everything to feel sure your wife loves you, and you can see in every expression of her face how much she loves you; yet, she is so unpresuming."

ERNEST:—" I guess I am not entirely indifferent to all those charms for I have been on the eve of proposing several times; but I would think I might regret it, for she does not quite come up to the standard of perfection."

HARRY:—"I presume you are right up to that standard point. You and I have always disputed on this question, so we will let it drop; but with all your wealth and its advantages, I would scorn to do so contemptable an act as you have perpetrated within that house. I swear, I thought you had got over that, or I should have warned her."

ERNEST:—"You take things terribly to heart. I came to have you go to the house with me as I thought I would say good bye to the girls; then, return and remain with you and leave in the morning, if you are not too angry with me. I tell you, Harry, women forget such things easier than you imagine."

HARRY:—Some women may, but not such noble women as Gertrude Mason. (rises.) I am ready to go to the house with you."

SCENE VII.

Mrs. Howrd's room, or dining room. Enter. Mrs. Howard.

HOWARD:—"I am glad Mr. Hilton feels as he does. I know Gertie is too proud to remain when she is not wanted, and her uncle turns rather a cold shoulder on her. She sees it, and that will draw her towards Loceno. I am glad, he believes so much in me. (*Enter Nora.*)

NORA:—"Mrs. Howard, there is a blind man and little girl at the door; they want to see you and won't take no for an answer."

HOWARD:—"What shall I do, Nora? See that none of the family are around, then send them in. (*Exit Nora.*) I intend this shall put an end to their coming. A person can not get so far away that a poor relative won't hang around them. My sister Elsie, was a lovely woman, but after death her family

was nothing to me. Mr. Hilton shall never know such people
are my relatives. (*Enter Harold and Minnie leading her
father; a little basket on her arm.*) Nora, bring my chair. (*Exit
Nora.*) So you are here again, are you? Is there anything
I can do to keep you away? (*Minnie seats her father in a chair*)

MINNIE:—" Aunt Hester, do not blame Papa for coming
here. He said he could not, but I was so tired and hungry,
and begged so long without eating anything, I couldn't go any
farther. Oh, Auntie! don't blame poor Papa."

HOWARD:—" See here, Minnie, don't repeat any of your
learned pitiful stories, for what may strike the sympathy of
others only angers me. I know you—what do you want?"

MINNIE: —" I am hungry, but Papa is very hungry! He
made me eat the last we had. (*arms around neck*) Poor Papa!
Oh, Auntie! you promised Mamma I should never want for
anything. O! my beautiful Mamma loved me so, and loved
poor Papa, too." (*sobs.*)

HOWARD:— " I don't care to witness any more of your fool-
ishness. I will give you some stuff from the kitchen if that
will get you away from here. Your beggardly appearance is
most shocking."

HAROLD:—(*Rising.*) " Hester, when I came in this room I
was faint with hunger, but this is misery which in its agony
drowns all thoughts of hunger. I feel strong, strong enough
to go and tell you what I have not forgotten before I leave
you."

HOWARD:—" Harold, I do not care to listen to you." (*Mo-
tions for them to go.(*

HAROLD:—" Remain where you are or the house shall know
you and your heartlessness."

HOWARD:—" Should you open your head to anyone I will
expose you, and then what would become of your child?""

HAROLD:—" Listen! When I married your sister I was
strong. I could see her life was all a devoted, ambitious
husband could make it. I tried to gratify her every wish, and
she was ever grateful, Oh, God! how happy I was! And
when little Minnie came to us we thought our happiness complete. You visited us then, praised our home, our baby, and
seemed to share in our happiness; but now I know the depth
of your affections. Elsie pitied you when you were left a
homeless widow. You were in want then. We had plenty
and we gave it to you; we did not call you a beggar. After

Elsie's death, strength and eyesight failed me. One misfortune followed another, until now my child, my poor motherless child, leads me about a beggar! a-a-blind beggar!''

HOWARD;—"Harold, don't you know if I was to tell a certain person where you were you would have a prison home the remainder of your life?"

HAROLD:—"Yes, but you know I am not guilty; you know I did not kill that man, although they have every reason to believe I did. If you were to swear would you say I was guilty?"

HOWARD:—"Yes, I would. Although I know you are not guilty, if you would bring out my right name, if you should ever let this family know me, I would swear that you killed that man; I would see you separated from Minnie, so be careful! No matter what may happen, keep silent, or your child shall be left at my mercy."

HAROLD:—"Then I would rather see her dead, Come, darling, we will go." (*Enter Mabel and Hofius.*)

MINNIE;—"Oh, Papa! I cannot walk, I am so hungry." (*Faintly. Harold tries to get Minnie away.*)

MABEL:—"Mrs. Howard, what does this mean?"

MINNIE:—"Papa, I am so hungry."

HOWARD:—(*taking hold of Minnie's arm.*) "I am trying to get these beggars out of here. (*to Minnie*) We do not make a practice of feeding beggars here." (*Enter Nora L.*)

MABEL:—"We never turn them away hungry. Little girl you shall have something to eat. Here, Nora, take them to the kitchen and give them all they want. (*Exit Harold, Minnie and Nora L.*) Mrs. Howard, don't ever turn away anyone from my father's home without food."

HOWARD:—"So long as I am house-keeper of this mansion I shall not be troubled to feed beggars. I shall not feed them."

MABEL:—"Mrs. Howard, to whom are you speaking? I am at home and you are not. If you wish to gain my father's love you must be kind to the poor."

HOFIUS:—"That's what's the matter! See how Uncle James took you in."

HOWARD:—"I was not a beggar, sir I have money of my own and I despise beggars."

MABEL:—"No matter how you may despise them, they must not leave our door, hungry Remember, you are my servant and must obey me."

HOFIUS:—"That's business!"(*Exit Mabel and Hofius at L.*)

HOWARD:—(*sitting.*) "Ah! 'tis indeed a bitter feeling to be so humbled. Yes, I am her servant and I must obey, for if I should not, I might loose this home and the opportunity of winning James Hilton. I will endure all, if I can win him with all his wealth,——I will endure it, but oh! how humiliating. I doubt that Harold and Minnie could have felt the humiliatiion I now feel. Ah! Mabel Hilton, I only endure this that I may live to see you thus tormented." (*Exit L.*")

SCENE VIII

Grove, Harry and Mabel walking toward front; Ernest and Gertie at distance.

MABEL:—"Now, Harry, you are jealous again, arn't you?" Forgive me this once and I will be more careful in the future. I do care for you and if there is anything more I can do to make you feel it, tell me."

HARRY:—"Mabel, tell me truly, don't you think you would love me more if I was not so infernally poor? if I had something else beside my practice to fall back on?"

MABEL:—"No, no! If you had all the money you want I shouldn't like you at all, so don't mention it again. I tell you, Harry, I can't endure so much of this jealousy!"

HARRY:—"I know I am foolish, but if you will forget this I will not do so again." (*Stoops to kiss her.*)

MABEL:—"No, no, Harry; Ernest and Gertie will laugh at us. Do you not think it a sudden notion, Ernest leaving so soon?"

HARRY:—"If he had left before it would have been better. I believe Gertrude loves Ernest and why has he trifled with one that is his superior? If there is any difference between them, he is the inferior. I think Gertie loves him and he has given her every reason to believe he returns it."

MABEL:—"I know she loves him, a somnambulist cannot keep her secrets. Yes she believes in him, he knows it, and if he should spurn her love I could never forgive him."

Ernest and Gertie rise, come to front; Mabel and Harry, back.

GERTIE:—"Ernest, I am quite surprised at your leaving so soon, a sudden freak, is it not?"

ERNEST :—" Not for me. I am nearly a freak at the best. I certainly find it unpleasant to leave a place where I have passed so many happy hours, and, Gertie, I am indebted to you for the greater amount of my summer pleasure."

GERTIE :—" Thanks, Ernest, I can return the compliment. I have known very little happiness since my mother's death and I shall hold these months in remembrance as nearer real happiness than I have experienced in years.

ERNEST:—" Do you think there is any real happiness, anything besides what wealth, fashion and gayety bestows?"

GERTIE :— " We that are born with hearts find happiness in living for those we love. There is real happiness in that, although I am not so irrational as to think we could exist without some obstacles."

ERNEST :—" No, the ignorant are the only ones continually happy. What think you of the quotation 'Ignorance is bliss' ?"

GERTIE :—" I prefer fruit from the tree of knowledge; I would rather suffer with my eyes open then be happy with them shut." (*both sit.*)

ERNEST :—" You are quite a little philosopher. I suppose, if I ever re-visit this city I will find you happy in some man's love, and there will be plenty to envy him." (*Takes off buttonhole boquet, and throws it in her lap.*)

GETIE :—" I do not picture anything of the kind for myself, but I shall be here to welcome you and yours, should you ever return."

ERNEST :—" Oh! I shall never marry, I never think of it. One I could call my wife I fear I shall never find, but if I should meet such a being, she would not listen to me, she would probably send me were the " Woodbine Twineth."

GERTIE :—" Excuse me, Ernest, if I ask a peculiar question, but idle curiosity prompts me to co so. Picture to me the woman you would be likely to wed."

ERNEST :—" Certainly ; I will describe her if my tongue is not too feeble. She must have a commanding figure, intellectual, educated, and all the accomplishments education can bestow. Drive fast horses, be and expert equestrian, row like a sailor, elegant in every move, no baby manners, nothing soft. She must be grand——so grand that all men will envy me, a lady whose very presence will silence all nonsense. What think you of the picture?"

GERTIE:—(*sadly*) "A very fascinating picture indeed; but I fear so fascinating a woman would be so enwrapped in the world's opinion she might neglect you."

ERNEST:—" I do not believe in this agonizing love, it does for the country. Too soft, you know."

GERTIE:—" Then is there no genuine affection but what we find in the country. I think to the contrary, there is no genuine love that does not come from an intellectual mind."

ERNEST:—"There is but very little feeling in these sighs, etc."

GERTIE:—" Pure, true love is not the off-spring of sighs, of prayers and entreaties, and all the small artillery of courtship There is pure genuine love; Ernest, you cannot mean what you say?"

ERNEST:—" Perhaps I am in the wrong; (*arises, looks at his watch.*) my time says I cannot remain much longer. It is always the same when I am in company with you. (*Gertie turns her head scornfully.*) I shall accompany Harry to his office this evening, and leave in the morning. (*Gertie rises, when he gives her his hand, the boquet falls to the ground.*)

GERTIE:—,' Mabel and I will miss you. You know I will miss you, as Mabel will spend much of her time with Harry."

EARNEST:—(*taking her hand.*) " I shall remember this summer and the many pleasant hours I have spent in your society. Remember, you have my best wishes farewell." (*Gertie bows, Ernest when half way to the back entrance, lifts hat to her and exit. Gertie raises both hands and watches him as he retreats.*)

GERTIE:—" Gone, gone without one word of love! Here is the end of all my summer dreams, not one word of love for me. I did not ask you to love me, but you taught me to love you. The lesson was easy, and oh! so sweet; why did you teach me to love you then push me aside as you would a worm that crawls in your path? Am I so worthless, you should cooly spurn my love? He has broken my heart, desolated my life, and must I carry this secret in my heart? Yes, though it eats my very existence. Oh, how I suffer! Ernest,——oh that that name! Linked with the happiest hours of my life and the bitterest; but I loved him, oh! how I loved him. (*picks up the little boquet, sobbing.*) Oh, what agony! (*kisses the flower and puts it in her bosom.*) Sleep there, little flower, and wither with my heart. I must dry these tears, these sobs, they must not know my suffering. To love as I have loved, and to have that love scorned, is enough for me, without the whole world knowing it. No, uncle must not see me weeping, I will sing. What shall I sing?"

(*Clasps hands over head, then drops together in front.*)

Sings I WOULD NOT FORGET THEE.

ACT II. SCENE. I.

Harold lying on an old couch; chamber poorly furnished.

HAROLD:—(*rising part way.*)   " Why doesn't Minnie come? She has been away a long time, something may have happened her."

Door opens, Minnie enters with basket on arm.

MINNIE:—"Papa, I am here.   I wish you could see the pieces of beef the butcher gave me, and here are lots of pieces of bread.   It will make a nice dinner for you and I know, dear Papa, you are hungry. (*she kisses him.*) I must get you something to eat. (*working busily*) I know you will get well and when I am a big girl we will have a nice time.   I'm not a bit tired, how do you feel, Papa?"

HAROLD:—"I think I am better and I am sure the dinner will make me entirely well.   My little daughter seems so happy." (*Harold lies down.*)

MINNIE:—" Yes, I am happy.   Aunt Hester gave me these pieces of bread."

HAROLD:—" Did she give you any money?"

MINNIE: —"Oh, yes!   I was in such a hurry to get your dinner I forgot all about it. (*counts money*) One, two. three, four, five, six, seven cents; and she said such mean things to me, but I don't care for that."

HAROLD :—" What did she say?"

MINNIE:—" I do not mind it, Papa, you always feel worse if I tell you, and she will be better by and by."

HAROLD:—"It will not affect me; tell me what she said."

MINNIE:—"She said: ' As long as you were sick you could not come there, and she was glad of it.   That she was coming here to-day to give you something more so I would stay at home.'   She pushed me down stairs and hurt my arm. (*Minnie sobs*) I know when I get big I won't have to ask her for anything."

HAROLD:—" Can it be possible so heartless a woman can be the sister of my wife, who was so loving, so kind?   Must I bear so much from one I have so often befriended?" (*Knock at door, Minnie opens it, Mrs. Howard enters.*)

HOWARD:—(*Lifting her dress from floor; brushing chair before seating herself.*) "Why, Harold, are you still in bed? I think a little exercise would be benificial; people that lie in bed and do nothing can never regain their strength."

HAROLD:—" Perhaps I could exercise if I had food to give me strength; but there are times when I have nothing and I cannot take food from my child."

HOWARD:—" Here is something I brought you. Take it, Minnie, (*gives Minnie package.*) I hope this will help toward keeping you till I can come again. (*to Minnie.*) Do not stop your begging, get all you can out of others, for I may not come again very soon. And, Harold, understand I do not want Minnie to come near me again; the first thing you know she will call me Auntie, and it may be the means of exposing me, and if I *am*, you shall suffer."

HAROLD:—" You ought to suffer, and were it not for leaving my child at your mercy, you should. They should know you, but that alone keeps me silent."

MINNIE:—" But, Auntie, if Papa should get awful sick, and nothing in the house to eat, couldn't I go if I was careful not to let anyone see me? Sometimes Papa is so hungry."

HOWARD:—(*Moving toward door.*) "No, you cannot, and remember it." (*Exit at door.*)

HAROLD:—" Minnie, has she gone?" (*Minnie sits by her father.*)

MINNIE:—" Yes, Papa."

HAROLD:—" Merciful Heaven! what have I done! what have I done to bring to bring this suffering upon myself and child, to bring my child to such misery? Minnie, how can you love me?"

MINNIE:—(*Arms encircle his neck.*) "Papa, I cannot help loving you, you are so good. Then, no one cares for me, no one cares whether I am hungry or not, no one but you, Papa."

HAROLD:—" Ah, darling, God knows I care for you; but to bring such suffering on my little Minnie, tender little lily—I should think you would curse me!"

MINNIE:—"Oh! Papa, don't talk so bad about yourself, when you are the sweetest Papa in the world."

HAROLD:—" My innocent child, without a mother's love, or mother's tender care—(*raises hands.*) Oh! Elsie, my wife, there is no room for us here, is there room for us there?" (*Falls over an couch, Minnie kneels at his feet.*) [*Scene closes in.*]

SCENE II.

Parlor in Hilton mansion; enter Hofius with book in hand, looking to see if any one is there.

HOFIUS:—" Well, the cats are away so the mouse will play. I will read as loud as I am a might to, no one will hear. (*turning leaves.*) Where is my place? I will show that professor that I haint going to be for ever and eternally learning this elocution business. I have plenty of poetry that I can repeat at a moment's notice. The teacher said it would be a fine thing for me if I could learn poetry easy. Yet I don't go much on sweet poetry. Darned if I can find that place! Guess I can repeat it any way. (*repeats.*) 'Hear me, ye walls, that echoed to the tread of either Brutus, once again I swear—— once again I swear—— (*looks for place*) I swear   I swear—— (*finds place*) I swear——' " (*Enter Mabel.*)

MABEL :—" Cousin Hofius, what are you swearing about ? "

HOFIUS :—(*Looks confused, then quotes in affecting style.*)

" I heard the rustle of your dress,
  I saw a shadow glide,
  And now I find,
     Oh, sweet the change !
  Dear Mabel by my side.

MABEL :—" The rose's red, the violet's blue,
  Sugar is sweet and so are you."

HOFIUS:—" Well, Mabel, I didn't get the start of you much, did I? You do know something about poetry, don't you ? "

MABEL :—" Yes, I used to read and recite at school."

HOFIUS:—" Say, Mabel, does that Harry Hanford mean anything serious by coming here? he acts as though he thought a good deal of you."

MABEL:—" I guess he likes me well enough, but there isn't anyone that cares very much of me."

HOFIUS:—" Yes, there is ! honestly, Mabel. Haint you got a feller ? "

MABEL :—" Do you mean a beau, Cos., a real, live, beau ? "

HOFIUS:—" Yes, sir, that's just exactly what I mean."

MABEL:—" No, Cos., I havn't."

HOFIUS:—" Now, aint you fooling me? "

MABEL:—" No, I havn't a real beau. I don't see why it is, but the boys don't seem to like me."

HOFIUS:—" Well, by Gosh, I like you! I don't care a cent if I did spark Sue Wright down in Squash Holler, a feller can't always stick to one girl. But if you hain't got a feller, I will just let her go to grass."

MABEL:—" But it may break her heart. I would always think of it and feel I was to blame."

HOFIUS:—" No, you needn't think that way at all. I never liked her any too well, any way. I wouldn't a took her to so many circuses and paring bees, but that blasted mother of hern makes a feller walk chalk. You see, it's like this: Sue Wright's mother, old Widder Wright's brindle cow was forever and eternally coming in our door yard, jump the fences and raise particular thunder, wherever she is, and our dog, Cudge, went for her. Over the fence the old cow went, and over the fence went Cudge after her, 'till he got hold her leg. She fell and crack went her leg! The Widder was driving the hogs around the corner and got there just in time to see old Brindle tumble. Now if I hadn't a laughed so loud it wouldn't a been so aggravating; but I laughed and she jawed. (Both laugh.) A few days after there was to be a big circus in town, a big show. I met the old lady and she says to me, says she, " Hof. Haskins, you can settle that cow question for about twenty-five dollars." Says I, " Mrs. Wright, that cow jumped into our yard." Says she to me, in that insinuating way, " You have got to 'tend to your knitting or you'll see." Now, I knew what she meant. You know the show was in town, as I said afore. The next day I asked Sue to go to the show, and the old woman was as good as pie."

MABEL:—"That was pretty bad for all of you, the widow and all."

HOFIUS:—" Yes, the old brindle limps, it kindy hurt her walk."

MABEL:—" I guess Sue will scarcely dare approach you on that subject again when you go home with your head filled with poetry, and your language one living, tangled mass of poems. I think a few of your readings will convince them of your importance; but I must go, and we will recite elocution lessons together." (Exit L.)

HOFIUS:—"Now, what a blasted fine girl she is, but she don't know much about Widder Wright's temper. I know enough to know that if she says old Brindle limps, it's time

for a feller about my size to scratch. Where is my lesson?
(*opens book.*) 'He king, my king, my king, when he is not
worthy to be called my dog—— (*looses place*) to be called my
dog—— (*finds place*) Forward, Slave, forward!,' That's jam up
talk, takes muscle to do this. (*reads*) Ah, Leonidas, to know
thee is to love thee.' " (*Nora enters L., seeing him she rushes
through room frightened.*)

NORA:—" Holy Mother ! "

HOFIUS:—" Nora frightens awful easy ; I wouldn't hurt her,
but here comes somebody." [*Exit L.*] (*Enter Mrs. Howard
and Loceno R.*)

LOCENO:—" I am glad to know Ernest has gone ; now, with
your help I may get her."

HOWARD:—" Yes, I am sure you can; she tries to conceal
her grief but she cannot. She will survive it soon, and I know
they are not engaged. Last night she walked and talked in
her sleep, and her mind is usually on Ernest, but it makes no
difference, she belongs to you and you shall have her." (*Enter
Hilton.*)

HILTON:—" Ah! I fear there is a secret and I must retire."

LOCENO:—" No secret from you, come in. Mr. Hilton, we
are willing you should know. Mrs. Howard has already told
you Gertie is my promised wife, she belongs to me and I want
her."

HOWARD:—" Gertie tried to get Ernest away from Mabel,
and I think if Gertrude would leave here, Ernest, on another
visit, would care for Mabel. Gertrude pushed herself ahead
and was determined to be in Mabel's way."

HILTON:—" I saw them together and was not pleased with
it at all. I am willing to do anything, for Mabel must marry
Ernest, I cannot have it any other way."

HOWARD:—" Yes, dear Mabel, so unselfish, so kind to Gertie,
awakes to find herself out in the cold. If I were you, James,
I would give her a holiday ; let her go to Banchester, among
Ernest's friends. That is, when Loceno and Gertie are married,
Mabel will be lonely. I sometimes fear the child is not well."

HILTON:—" Mrs. Howard, how can you take such an interest
Mabel when she is often abusive to you ?. You shall be repaid
for your untiring patience; and, my dear Hester, do not
worry so much about Mabel ; she is young and will be different
in time. I thank you for being so kind. Whenever you need
my assistance you have only to say the word. You must

excuse me at present." (*Exit L.*)

LOCENO:—"Ah, it would do my heart good to see you mistress of this mansion!"

HOWARD:—"I hope to be some day. When I am, saucy Mabel shall not interfere, and I will rid the house of that elocutionary-tragical nephew. If I can only get Gertie and Mabel away from here I am sure of winning Mr. Hilton."

LOCENO:—"I am sure you can. I am sure I can. (*Rising.*) Time has passed rapidly, I became so interested in Gertie. (*Exit L.*) Good night, Mrs. Howard."

HOWARD:—"Good night. James Hilton is on my side. Gertie is such a timid being, Loceno can frighten her so she would feel compelled to accept him. When I am Mrs. Hilton, Harold and Minnie can have what belongs to them; they have learned to suffer; I have not and shall not. (*Looks at watch.*) 'Tis time and past time for retiring. (*Exit L.*)

SCENE III.

Two chairs and ottoman—Night—Moonlight—Soft music—Gertie moves in slowly, seeming to push objects from before her.

GERTIE:—"O, how the air oppresses me! What clings to me so closely? why, mother, was it your embrace? Oh, mother, am I with you? O! how beautiful! Do not leave me, mother. Heaven! oh, how beautiful! Mother, this must be a dream, and must I awake, (*Reaches out hand then draws back suddenly*) oh, I must not try to touch them lest I awaken. Mother, keep near me, do not leave me. Is heaven always so beautiful, (*smiles*) so, so beautiful; mother, keep near me. No, no, not now, for, mother, see you Ernest? he is waiting for me. I am weary, oh, so weary. O! how beautiful is heaven. Mother, keep near me, do not touch me lest I awaken. How strange I feel! Ernest, mother, mother, Ernest. Beautiful home."

MABEL:—[*Enters: Gertie listening.*] "Gertie, dear! (*Tries to awaken her*) Gertie!"

GERTIE:—"Mother, 'tis Ernest calling me—yes, I hear."

MABEL:—"Gertie, dear, do awaken; you are dreaming again."

GERTIE:—"Oh, Ernest, do not tell me I am dreaming, 'tis so sweet to be near you. Hush! listen! Loceno is in the thicket, I know he is there, I heard him muttering to himself."

MABEL:- "Gertie, Loceno is not here. Gertie!"

GERTIE:—"Hush, speak not so loud, he will hear you and may harm you. Hush!"

MABEL:—"Gertie, do awake. See, the moon is coming in. 'Tis chilly here, we must return to our bed. Come, Gertie."

GERTIE:—(*Leaning on Mabel.*) "O, Ernest, I am so weary."

MABEL:—"What am I to do! Darling Gertie, with a heart too pure, too true for Ernest Vaughn, and yet he has spurned her love. Must her days be spent in misery, her nights torn in anguish? O! Ernest Vaughn, I curse the day when you crossed our threshold. If you could suffer as she suffers—must she endure this?"

GERTIE:—"Oh! (*Reaches forth hands.*) Oh!"

MABEL:—"Gertie, are you awake?" [*Kisses her.*]

GERTIE:—[*Sobbing.*] "Why must I awake, why must I awake to life and misery!"

MABEL:—"Gertie, we must not stay here, 'tis so late. Do you know where you are?"

GERTIE:—"Too well I know where I am. This has all been a dream. (*sobs*) 'Twas a sweet dream. Ernest and mother! Oh, that my life could be one long dream!"

MABEL:—"Come, Gertie, do not mourn so, it grieves me to hear it. I am tired and sleepy, will you come now?"

GERTIE:—"No, no, I cannot sleep now. The moonlight is so beautiful. No, I cannot sleep."

MABEL:—"Is the remainder of your life to be spent in this way, mourning for Ernest Vaughn when he is so unworthy?"

GERTIE:—"Oh, Mabel, say not that he is unworthy of me; he is worthy of anyone. I am unlike his ideal of a woman."

MABEL:—"But he liked you, he knew what he was doing. He is sufficiently intelligent to realize—I would like to know what his ideal is."

GERTIE:—"He told me, Mabel."

MABEL:—"He told you? The impudent fellow! What did he say?"

GERTIE:—"I asked him to tell me. He says she must be a woman worthy a crown; she must be good-looking, dark hair and eyes; must dance, row, ride, drive; must excel in all feminine graces and, in fact, do many things that men do. Also, a woman that men will rave about; no *baby* manners; a grand lady whose very presence will silence all nonsense. Beautiful picture is it not, Mabel?"

MABEL:—" Yes, a nice picture. But when he meets such a woman as that she will probably drive right by. Let me tell you what came into my mind when you were repeating his words: You can be all of that if you choose."

GERTIE: —" I be such a woman as that ? "

MABEL:—" Certainly. You have a determination within you if you would only bring it out. You can drive, ride and row comparatively well, and with the inner determination of being and doing all he has spoken of I know you can succeed. Dōn't you think so?"

GERTIE:—" I could do many of these things, but not all."

MABEL:—" Yes, you could. You are tall, beautiful, educated, and one year at Weed's School for Out-door Accomplishments for Young Ladies would place you where he would see men rave over you, but he, most of all, as he knows the purity of the heart within."

GERTIE:—" Perhaps I can do this, yet, Mabel, I could never marry Ernest now, he left me so unfeelingly, so heartlessly."

MABEL:—" No, no, dear, certainly not; or, you could do as you please when the time comes. But I should let him know tnat such a woman can exist, and that such a one he cannot possess on very short notice. So far as soft nothings are concerned you never indulged in anything silly. He has tried to crush every spark of sweet affection."

GERTIE:—" Crushed! Yes, I believe I shall live to see the time when my affection for him shall have crumbled entirely away. To live for revenge will crush the 'babyishness,' as he terms it, in me."

MABEL:—" I am glad you have stopped mourning. Dear, dear Gertie, to see you happy will make me happy; but to give up to mourn all your days for him would be a life poorly spent. Oh Gertie, cousin, dear, do you know how much I love you?"

GERTIE:—[Pushing her away.] " Mabel, do not unnerve me. (sobs) I know that you love me, you are the only one that does, and I worship you for it. But go, Mabel, go to your room, I will soon follow. (Mabel retires through curtains.) Ernest may forsake me, but Mabel loves me; Uncle Hilton turns against me, and Mabel clings the closer. Uncle Hilton forgets all when I most need sympathy. No one but an orphan can have sympathy. No home, no father, no mother, oh, how we hunger for affection from those around us. No one to protect us, do we not deserve pity, do we not deserve sympathy when we would give our life to fall asleep, one night, with a father's tender blessing, a mother's warm kiss? Oh, I am so chilly. Has the beautiful morn deserted my chamber? Is

it morning?   Oh, everything seems so strange!   I alone, alone, my
brain whirls!   Mabel! Mabel!" [*Mabel draws curtains around
her, winds around 'till comes to curtain and sinks.*]

SCENE IV.

Parlor—Enter Nora, dusting.

NORA—" I'm glad to git me work done before that crazy cousin
comes.   I wonder where Miss Mabel and Miss Gertie can be.
Slaping still the beauta; may they slape swately is the wish of Nora.
It nearly drives me wild to see that crazy cousin, Hofius, he scares
the life out o' me.   Nary a night have I slept a good slape. (*Hofius
appears at door unobserved by her.*) I try and try to slape, but
no slape comes to me eyes for the dreamin' o' him.   Yes, I'se fraider
than death itself o' him. (*Nora observes him.*) Holy Mother, I am
kilt now! (*Sits on carpet.*) I couldn't walk a peg if I tried; not if I
died the next minnit; so very wake, you know.   I'm all gone; no
brith in me bones."

HOFIUS:--[*Laughing.*] " I will help you. Nora.   Are you sick,
eh?"

NORA:—" Oh. yis, I shouldn't wonder.   I'm almost gone wid a
faint stomach." [*Hofius helps her up, she looks frightened.*]

HOFIUS:—" I will help you up slicker 'n a fiddle." [*Goes to door
when Hofius shuffles feet to frighten her.*]

NORA:—" Oh. Merciful Powers, I'm dead agin!"

HOFIUS:--" Dead again, Nora?   Then crawl off and bury yourself   I must read. (*Commences to read and Nora crawls off
frightened.   Recites this; opens book.*)

> Wild was the night, yet a wilder night
> Hung 'round the soldier's pillow,
> Be not like dumb driven cattle,
> Be a hero in the strife.

Guess I had better look, that don't sound good.   Poetry does for
girls but not for men.   Brutus and Cæsar, etc., is the kind of a man
I am.   Muscle in that—" [*Enter Hilton and Mrs. Howard.*]

HILTON:—" I was sure I had educated Mabel to be kind to the
poor; I am sorry she should turn against them; I hope you will
teach her better.   Well, Hofius, how is elocution prospering?"

HOFIUS:--" I tell you, Uncle Jim, I am getting elocution down to
about as fine a point as it can be got.   I take to it like a duck takes
to water." [*Enter Gertie and Mabel. Gertie goes to Hofius.*]

MABEL:—" Why, Papa, I have been looking all over for you."

HILTON:—" I presume so. Small demand on my pocket-book, is it not? "

MABEL:—" Yes. Gertie and I are going to the opera, Wednesday evening; we would like you to accompany us if you will, but if you cannot we know of one who can fill the place admirably. And I want a new opera cape and a new hat or Gertie will be ashamed to go with me; my cloak looks shabby."

HILTON:—" Then get one, by all means."

MABEL:—" Oh, you are the boss Papa."

HOWARD:—" I should think extra clothes were superfluous; such pretty faces ought to carry you through."

MABEL:—" Well, as cousin Hof. says, I want it just the samee."

HILTON:—" Mabel, I am shocked! Arn't you ever going to possess any dignity, any respect for others? "

MABEL:—" Dear me, I forget! I'll commence all over again and and try to be careful."

HOFIUS:—" I know something that will cure you."

MABEL:— " Do you? Tell me, and I will take the dose, whatever it may be."

HOFIUS:—" You don't take it; it takes you."

MABEL:—" It takes me? Does it wear a hat? Carry a cane? "

HILTON:—" Your conduct is ridiculous!"

HOFIUS:—" Pshaw! she isn't half so bad as she was down in the country. Now you wouldn't believe it, but I'll be darned if sae didn't— (*Mabel scowls,*) if—if—it don't rain awfully down on the farm; makes things look as green –"

HILTON: -(*Smiling,*) Yes, I presume so. I have heard that Mabel carried on terribly; climbed cherry trees and straw-stacks and—"

HOFIUS:—" You bet she could and quicker than I? but there was one thing I could do, beat her on a race to catch (*Mabel scowls.*) to catch, we'd catch the infernalest colds you ever heard of after the rainy spells." [*Mabel laughs.*]

HILTON:—[*Smiles.*] " Mrs. Howard, we will go into the library. Who is to be your escort, Mabel? "

MABEL:—" Harry Hanford."

HILTON:—" Is that another lover of Gertrude's? "

GERTIE:—" Uncle, how can you be so unkind? "

MABEL:—" Why. Papa, how can you speak so unkind to Gertie when I love her so! "

HILTON:—" Yes, but you are loving your enemy."

MABEL:—" Never mind, Gertie, that woman is the cause of these remarks."

GERTIE:—" I understand; I am no longer a baby." [*Exit R.*]

MABEL:—" What a wicked world! Those who are the best fare the worst."

HOFIUS:--" You are right, and it is my private opinion that old Madam Howard has got enough downright cussedness in her to supply a nation; don't you think so."

MABEL:—" Yes, sir, I do. Say, Coz., I thought you wanted me to recite those lines with you."

HOFIUS:—" Yes, course I do. I'd thought I'd ask you about it, but, darn my buttons, if I didn't kind a hate to."

MABEL:—[*Taking book.*] " Let me take the book and recite it as I was taught, then you may imitate it; (*reads*) ' Beautiful visions I see before me; all is calm and serene; but when I turn and look, O, agony of the past! ' How do you like that? "

HOFIUS:--" That's boss."

MABEL:—" Remember the gestures, and when you turn, turn quickly. Now try it."

HOFIUS:--[*Takes book: awkward gestures.*] " ' Beautiful visions I see afore me; all is cam and serene; but when I turn—" [*Turns and falls; Mabel laughs while he lies there.*]

MABEL:—[*Laughingly.*] Cousin, we will have to have a curtain for extra occasions. (*Laughs*) Oh, dear! " [*Hofius still lies on floor.*]

HOFIUS:—" Keep right on laughing; laugh if you want to. (*Sits up*) I'll give up the business, go right home, won't stay any longer; keep right on laughing. Mabel. I'll go right home and marry Sue Wright, to-morrow, and I'll let that old mother of hern boss me, too. Don't stop laughing for me. You knew darned well I would tumble down, didn't you? "

MABEL:—" No I—I did not."

HOFIUS:—" Yes you did. Sue Wright's good 'nough for me anyhow." [*Looks slily at Mabel.*]

MABEL:—" You want to make me jealous by talking of Sue. I was laughing to see what a teacher I'd make "

HOFIUS:—" You can't fool this chicken, I know something I guess. Sue Wright is good enough for me. Sue haint to be sneezed at. She could just throw a cart load of city girls over her left shoulder and carry them to market for second-hand rubbish."

MABEL:—[*Pouting.*] " Hof., you don't like me at all."

HOFIUS:—" You know darn well I do; but, as the saying goes, ' never put off 'till to-morrow what you can do to-day.' "

MABEL:—" What do you mean by that."

HOFIUS:—" Just this · If you laugh at me again I shall not put Sue off 'till to-morrow but go and marry her to-day. If you liked me as well as Gertie does her feller you'd sing something pitiful like she did. I don't wonder that the boys don't like you. Why don't you sing something kindy soft about me if you like me so tarnel well."

MABEL:—" Often have I, in the still hours of evening, sat me down in the parlor and scratched the strings of my guitar and wondered where you were, like the twinkle twinkle little star. (*Voices heard without.*) Listen! I thought I heard Mrs. Howard and Loceno; if they are together it means something. Go and let me listen. I am afraid for Gertie and Papa." [*Exit Hofius: Mabel conceals herself; Enter Mrs. Howard and Loceno.*]

HOWARD:—" I have been studying this over carefully; you know she intends going soon to Prof. Weed's seminary, down the Hudson river, about 80 miles from here, and you must begin to attend to things. There is to be a grand concert at Park Centre, to-morrow evening. They are very elegant affairs. Gertie wants to go, so Mr. Hilton is going to send her with one of the gentlemen from the bank to accompany her there. You can meet her when she steps out of the carriage, conduct her to the hotel; the carriage will return and she will be left alone at your mercy. She is timid, you threaten her with the promises of her dying mother, and you will win. But for fear that does not, I can arrange something that will. Mr. Hilton is Gertie's guardian. Gertie knows nothing of the disposal of her money. You fix up some paper, I can write like him so I will sign his name to it and convey the idea to her that this belongs to you should she refuse. That will frighten her as she is too proud to be dependent on anyone. You could not do this with many women, but Gertie is a truthful, timid, trusting girl. Such people never suspect, and can be frightened into anything. Mabel will be obliged to remain at home to-morrow evening as Mr. Hilton has told her some of his friends will be here and she must help entertain; so Gertie will be alone. I believe you can have your

Gertie and the money."

LOCENO:—" Yes, Mrs. Howard, I want both. I love Gertie madly, but her money is quite acceptable. They all think I teach for pastime, but the money never comes amiss."

HOWARD:—" I believe everything is arranged satisfactorily." [*rises.*]

LOCENO:—" I am sure we will be happy. I shall look for and be prepared for her to-morrow night."

HOWARD:—" And you shall not be dissapointed, but I will see you once more before you leave." [*Both exit L.*]

MABEL:—[*Comes from hiding place.*] " So this is the scheme is it. Oh, how can Papa be duped by such a woman, yet he believes her instead of me. (*Enter Hofius.*) Hof., where is Gertie? "

HOFIUS:—" Coming in here she said. Say, did it pay you to listen; I guess you didn't hear anything good about yourself, did you? " [*Enter Gertie.*]

MABEL:—" No, I did not. Oh, Gertie, I have something terrible to tell you, and we may need help. I will make a confidant of Hofius. Coz., will you stand by us and not reveal a word we may tell you? "

HOFIUS:—[*Putting hands in pockets.*] " Say, do you take me for a darn tattler? No, course I wont tell, no siree! "

MABEL:—" That Mrs. Howard has made Papa believe that Gertie wants to marry Loceno. They are going to have you go to the Park concert. I want you, Gertie, to agree to everything Papa says; act delighted if necessary. When the carriage comes I will go. (*Shows pistol.*) I have this and can use it, can't I, Hof.? "

HOFIUS:—" You bet."

GERTIE:—" I cannot see you go alone. If anything should happen you have a father who cares for you, I have no one who would miss me. I must go."

MABEL:—" You shall not go. The man who owns the hotel is Papa's old friend. I am safe, but I want Papa to know that I understand this, I want him to know."

GERTIE:—" If you wish to go to convince your father, why, I will consent."

MABEL:—" That's a good girl. Come, Hof." [*Exit Hof. & Mabel*]

GERTIE:—" They ought not to be in so great a hurry to dispose of me. They cannot compel me to marry Loceno, no never. I shall soon leave for my school. 'Tis a bitter thought to know that my uncle wishes me here no longer, but to know that uncle would be willing, or even suffer me to marry Loceuo, is worse than all. Yet, he says and does all through the love of Mrs. Howard. Yes, uncle, I forgive you, for love is a mighty mystery, we are its slaves when in its coils. Oh—'[*Enter Mrs. Howard.*]

HOWARD:—" Oh, Miss Gertie, why so despondent, happiness awaits you." [*Gertie looks at her then turns back when answering*]

GERTIE:—" Are you sure that any happiness awaits me? I wish I could feel that any happiness awaits me. Tell me, is there anything new to disturb the monotony? "

HOWARD:—" Yes, your uncle has made arrangements for you to attend the Park Theatre concert. You will be accompanied by one of the men in the bank. Now, do you not think that happiness? "

GERTIE:—" I am extremely happy. I will prepare myself. How kind of uncle, how thoughtful, how very kind."

HOWARD:—" Your uncle will send a carriage for you at seven. I am sorry that Mabel cannot accompany you, but Mr. Hanford and others will be here this evening." [*Exit.*]

GERTIE:—" Oh, I can go alone for the sake of attending the concert. (*Enter Hilton R.*) Uncle, I've heard of my concert trip, is your driver safe? "

HILTON:—" Perfectly. I hope you will have a pleasant time."

GERTIE: —" I expect to have a delightful time."

HILTON:—" Yes, here is the carriage; you will have a delightful time." [*Exit L.; Enter Mabel showing pistol; dressed togo out*]

MABEL:—" I will have lots of fun."

GERTIE:—" Dear Mabel, I am so afraid you will have trouble. It seems a desperate thing for you to do."

MABEL:—" Never fear; I'm not afraid of anybody, don't care for anybody, do I, Hof.? "

HOFIUS:—" No; that's the trouble, you don't care for anybody, no, course you don't, but I wish you did."

MABEL:—[*Looking out of window.*] " There's the carriage; come Hof., I must hurry and be sly." [*Exit Gertie R. Mabel and Hofius L. Enter Nora arranging chairs.*]

NORA:—" There is mischief somewhere, mischief up someplace. Ah, Mrs. Howard, ye are of the meanest, slyest; ah, ye are at the bottom of this." [*Enter Mrs. Howard and Mr. Hilton.*]

HOWARD: —" Nora, has Miss Gertie gone? "

NORA:—" Yis. mum, the carriage jist drav down the strate."[*Exit Left.*]

HILTON:—" I hope Gertie will have a good time. If she can endure him she is welcome to him."

HOWARD:—" Of course she scarcely expected to meet him so soon. Then she will be out of Mabel's way when Ernest comes, if he ever does."

HILTON:—" Yes, if he ever does! Oh, that Gertie should come between them when you had told her I was so interested in Ernest and Mabel. She is very unlike her father and mother or she could not have done so. 'Tis strange! "

HOWARD:—" I will admit it is strange. But, still waters run deep.' "

NORA:—" Mr. Hanford is in the drawing room."

HILTON: —" Show him in. (*Mrs. Howard rises to go.)* Mrs. Howard, please remain, you are acquainted with Mr. Hanford. Woerever I am I am happier by having you present. I presume Harry is delighted to know that business will bring him here often as Mabel's society is very agreeable. Oh, well; young folks ought not te be blamed when old folks do the same, eh? " [*Enter Harry L. all bow, shake hands, etc., Mrs. Howard places chair.*]

HOWARD:—" Please be seated. Mr Hanford." [*Enter Hofius whistling.*]

HILTON: —" Mr. Hanford, my nephew, Mr. Haskins." [*Hofius shakes heartily and long.*]

HOFIUS:—" How do you do, sir. I'm glad to make your acquaintance. I've saw a good many folks since I have been visiting at uncle Jim's. (*Tips back in chair.)* Haint this been an awful sozzly day though? "

HARRY:—" Yes, rather disagreeable."

HILTON:—" Were you successful in finding those papers, Mr. Hanford? "

HARRY:—" My partner has nearly all of them now."

HOFIUS:—" Did you say your name was Hanford? "

HARRY:—" Yes, sir."

HOFIUS:—" The name Hanford is very common to me, but between you and me I never knew a Hanford yet that was worth powder to blow them away. (*All look astonished.)* That is, I never happened to saw one. But I don't mean to say that you are not a square feller." [*Hilton interrupting.*]

HILTON:—" I fear, Mr. Hanford, that you will find some difficulty in arranging that matter; 'tis quite an affair."

HOFIUS:—" Yes, the name Hanford sounds natural. Why, you are Harry Hanford, haint you? "

HARRY:—" Yes, that is my name."

HILTON:—" Hofius, I think you are a little too curious."

HOFIUS:—" Well, I was just trying to find out something."

GERTIE:—[*Enter Gertie, all look confused.*] " Mr. Hanford, Mabel expected to be here, but decided to go to the concert in my place. She wished me to apologise to you for her absence. (*Hilton rises; Hofius turns to audience and laughs.*) I tried to persuade her to remain but she was determined to go. Why so agitated, uncle? "

HILTON:—" My God! what will become of her. Mrs. Howard, what is to be done? Hof., order a carriage immediately, let me go to her. Loceno, in his anger, would show no mercy. Heavens! " [*Exit Hofius.*]

HARRY:—" Mr. Hilton, tell me where to go, give me a horse and saddle. I can go better than you. Where is she? "

HILTON:—" She is at Park Centre hotel and will meet Loceno Diluppa there; such a man as he would not hesitate to do anything when angry. Take the best horse, Hanford, I will follow in the carriage." [*Hofius heard without.*]

HOFIUS:—" This way, uncle." [*Exit Hilton and Harry.*]

HOWARD:—" I thought you were going."

GERTIE:—" No, I decided to let Mabel go in my place as the pleasure was *too* great; I was afraid I could not appreciate it. 'Tis strange that uncle James should be so exercised over this since you and he were *so* sure of my having a pleasant evening." [*Enter Hof laughing.*]

HOWARD:—" This is very strange! "

GERTIE:—" Yes, indeed, this is very *very* strange."

HOFIUS:—" You'r right, Madam Howard, this is darned strange."

HOWARD:—[*To Hofius.*] " Did you know that Mabel was going? "

HOFIUS:—" Ask me no questions and I'll tell you no lies."

HOWARD:—" This is very strange I must say." [*Exit.*]

HOFIUS:—" This bothers the old girl, don't it? She thinks we can't saw through anything."

GERTIE:—" Hof., I am so nervous, I am so afraid that something may harm Mabel. [*Hofius goes to her.*] I am glad you are here?"

Hofius:—" So am I. You aint 'fraid when I am here, be you, Gertie?"

Gertie:—" No. What a cruel looking woman Mrs. Howard is. I hope Mabel will come unharmed as I go to my school to-morrow."

Hofius;—" Well now you need not fret over Mabel, she is all right; but I wish you would kind a look after me."

Gertie:—[*Rises and laughs.*] " Come in the library with me, Hofius, I am terribly nervous. (*Hofius wants to be coaxed.*] Hof. please come with me. I dislike to go alone. Arn't you coming?"

Hofius:—" Who would you rather have go with you than me?"

Gertie:—" No one, no one." [*Both exit arm in arm.*]

SCENE V.

Room in hotel; Loceno pacing to and fro.

Loceno:—" It is time for Gertie to be here, but they have probably driven slow. What a lovely wife she will make; how I will be envied. Oh, if she only loved me as I do her. If she does not readily consent I will have a dark home for her till she does. Yet I will not harm her, I could not harm her, she is too lovely. But she shall marry me, I have everything in readines. (*Goes to door.*) You are there are you, boys. (*two answer yes. Enter Mabel closely veiled.*) Oh, my dear Gertie, you did not expect to see me did you!" [*Mabel uncovers face.*]

Mabel:—" Oh yes, but did you expect to see me?"

Loceno:—[*Steps back*] " Heavens! how came you here—why—how—"

Mabel:—" I came in the carriage, the same way Gertie would have come. I enjoy the joke more than Gertie would. Come, Loceno, take me to the concert, I am all ready."

Loceno:—" What under heavens brought you here. (*advancing toward her.*] How did you know I was here? Who told you? Tell me!"

Mabel:—" I wanted to go to the concert. Ha! ha!"

Loceno:—" Who told you I was here! I could crush you." [*Goes toward her.*]

Mabel:—" Stand where you are. You can talk to me if you want to, you know I am not afraid of you."

Loceno:—" Do you suppose a woman's threats would effect me?

Your father, Mrs. Howard and all are conspiring against me. What a fool they have made of me. How did you know I was here? O! I could crush you."

MABEL:—[*Taking out pistol,*] " I am pleased to see you but don't come too near."

LOCENO:—" Do not further taunt me or you shall have the fate of Gertrude had she been stubborn. Who told you I was here? Who told you I was here, I ask again. Do you still refuse to tell me who told you? I am not alone, Miss Mabel, I have plenty of help at a moment's notice. Why do you not answer? " [*Goes toward her.*]

MABEL:—" My only answer is : This shows no mercy."

LOCENO:—[*Stepping back, tapping on door when two masked men rush in and cover her with blanket which bears her to floor*] " Hold her tight, she is armed.

MABEL:—" Help! Help! "

LOCENO:—" It will do you no good to cry, no one can hear you."

MASKED MEN:—" Shall we carry her to the place you directed? "

LOCENO:—" Not yet, hold her tight, she is armed. Now, my fine captured bird, tell me who told you I was awaiting Gertrude."

MABEL:—" Help! help! "

LOCENO:—" Your voice isn't loud enough to pass beyond this wall. Are Mrs. Howard and Mr. Hilton conspiring against me? [*Mabel fires pistol. Enter Harry. Knocks Loceno down.*]

HARRY:—" What does this mean? Where is Mabel? "

MABEL:—" Harry, is this you? [*Masked man & Harry wrestle, Harry falls. Mabel winds blanket around head of masker. Loceno starts to go forward but falls back. Harry remains unconscious. Masked man picks up Mabel and grasps Loceno's hand.*] Help! help! Oh, Harry! oh Harry." [*Mabel is wrapped in blanket to tighten arms. Loceno walks feebly.*]

MASKED MAN:—" Come or we shall be caught. [*Enter Hilton and two officers.*]

HILTON:—" Oh, my child! Drop her instantly."

First officer binds masked man, second officer grasps Loceno. Mabel falls to floor. Harry rises and falls to floor again. Mabel throws up arms.

MABEL:—" Oh, Papa." [*Faints in his arms.*]

HILTON:—" Loceno, what have you been doing? "

LOCENO:—" You sent Mabel here instead of Gertrude; you and Mrs. Howard are conspiring against me. You have lied to me."

HILTON:—" Hold, hold, sir, you are in the hands of these men. Mabel, are you better? "

MABEL:—" Yes, but I am so nervous, so frightened.

HILTON:—" Harry, how does your head feel? "

HARRY:—" I am better now.

LOCENO:--" I would not wrong Mabel, I only tried to have her tell me how she happened to know I was here. Some day I shall know what this means."

HILTON: —" Loceno, we did not know that Mabel intended coming here. (*Mabel goes to Harry.*) They must have planned it. I am sorry it has turned out so unsatisfactorily to you, and will give you money to return to your former place. I will give it to you willingly."

LOCENO:—" I know I need money, but oh, heavens! must I go and leave Gertrude? " [*Mabel and Harry stand left of front.*]

HILTON: —" I can see no other way   There is no use, she will never marry you although you are good enough for her." [*Mabel shudders.*]

LOCENO:—" Am I good enough for her?   I was good enough for her money but not for Gertie." [*Hilton gives money.*]

HILTON:—" Here is all the money you need.   Take it and promise never to return.   Do you promise? "

LOCENO:—" I do.   I would not take the money but necessity compels me to." [*Puts money in pocket.*]

HILTON:—" There will only be more of such trouble if you remain, so be good as your word and keep away from us."

LOCENO:—" I will never return. [*Steps toward Mabel.*] Miss Mabel, will you take my last words to Gertie? Tell her farewell; tell her I would suffer keenest agony for years for one sweet smile as I leave her forever. Her name shall be last on my lips when dying. Tell her good bye. I am ready to go." [*Exit Loceno and officers L.*]

HILTON:—" Come, we must go. (*Harry throws cape around Mabel.*) Mabel, how could you do so rash a thing? "

MABEL:—I am all right; but oh, what would cousin Gertie have have done? My trouble is nothing compared to what poor cousin Gertie would have suffered. I am thankful is was I, but oh, what a shameful trick! " [*Exit all R.*]

SCENE VI.

Parlor—Hofius with book in hand reading.

Hofius:—[*Reads.*]
  Great and understanding nation,
    Bear with one, whose humble pen,
  Sends this hearty commendation
    Flying through the mouths of men.
Let me turn to something else. (*Read.*) 'The village sewing society.'
    Miss Jones is late again to-day,
      I'd be ashamed if it was me.
I can't read, course I can't read. A feller can't when he is dead in love with three girls. Out of the three which shall it be. [*Tragically.*] Out of the three, which shall it be? " [*Enter Gertie.*]

Gertie:—" Reading again, are you? I wish I could read or do anything, I am so nervous, I think of Mabel continually."

Hofius:—" Nervous, why that's what all old maids say. You don't intend to be an old maid do you. Gertie? "

Gertie:—" Yes. I do."

Hofius:—" Sure as you live and breathe aint you ever going to get married? "

Gertie:—" No. I shall not."

Hofius:—" That lets me out."

Gertie: —" I hope Mabel is all right."

Hofius:—" You bet she is all right: needn't fret about her, she was prepared; she haint none of your caterpillar kind."

Gertie:—" I am glad to hear you speak so assuringly. She must come in time to see me at the landing. I could not leave without seeing her."

Hofius:—" Don,t you suppose that anybody else hates to see you go? I know a feller that will watch your boat 'till it gets clean out of sight."

Gertie:—[*Thinking.*] " How can I say farewell to uncle Hilton after he has done as he has? "

Hofius:—" There it goes again. Don't you hate to say good bye to any one else? " [*Enter Harry and Mabel L.*]

Gertie:—" Dear Mabel, I am so glad you are here and safe. too. Now I am happy."

MABEL :—" Yes, Gertie, I have had a terrible time; I'm so tired. Come into my room. Harry, you and Hofius must excuse us as we must prepare for Gertie's departure; you know she leaves for her school to-day, and the boat comes in at three o'clock. Be sure to be at the landing, and come a little before time." [*Exit L.*]

HOFIUS :—[*Confidentially.*] " Well, I suppose you have had a devil of a time. I suppose Mabel told you all about the fuss. (*Harry remains silent; Hofius brings chair close to Harry.*) You needn't be so darned fraid to talk to me about it, I know the whole business and I told the girls that I wouldn't tell and darned if I will. (*Sits back.*) So if you have anything to say, spit her out."

HARRY :—" There is not much to say, but it was fortunate for me that Mr. Hilton came in as he did or they might have used me up." [*Enter Mr. Hilton and Mrs. Howard.*]

HILTON :—" Hofius. did you know that Mabel was going last night? " [*Hofius acts confused.*]

HOFIUS :—" She is always doing something when you don't expect her to. Lord sake, no one knows just what she is going to do, but darned if she don't always come out boss. I haint ever saw such a girl."

HILTON :—" Then you did not know she was going? "

HOFIUS :—" She's a surpriser; always surprising some one. [*Looks at watch.*] Harry, it will soon be time to go and see Gertie leave, and come with me, there is something Gertie wanted us to do before she left."

HILTON :—" Is Gertie going to-day, going without saying anything to me? " [*Hofius and Harry start L.*]

HOFIUS :—" I can't say as to that, but she is going all the same." [*Both exit.*]

HOWARD :—" Your nephew is quite original."

HILTON :—" Yes, and fully as disagreeable. So Gertrude is going. I know I do not deserve a parting word from her as she is satisfied that I was in the plot."

HOWARD :—" I tried to convince her that you never suspected anything wrong, I thought it best as you were her uncle."

HILTON :—" You are kind to think of it, but I am sure she believes me guilty, as I am. Gertrude's mother was my only sister, a lovely woman. Gertrude resembles her; that same sweet, forgiving disposition."

HOWARD :—" Ah, no, not a very good disposition to plan the seperation of Mabel and Ernest. Had her mother lived she might have been a better girl, but, as it is, I shall stand by Mabel."

HILTON:—" I am sorry that Getie has done as she has. Her father was my main support when I started out in business. I owe everything to them; my life to her mother's tender care, my fortune to her father's kindness and instruction. No matter what she has done it is my duty to go and bid her good bye." [*Exit.*]

HOWARD:—" What a conscientious man he is; that is why it is so hard to disbelieve in others. I am, indeed. left alone; I must rely upon myself. Loceno gone and dare not return; Gertie away, too' Now I must try to seperate Mabel and her father; convince him that she has no affection for him, but for others. I'll make things so disagreeable, and I'll convince him that Mabel is at the bottom of it; and if I can get her away I can soon win him, and win him I must. I was never beaten yet when I started out to do anything mean. It's in me to conquer." [*Exit R.*]

SCENE VII.

Rocks and river—Mabel and Gertie standing at top—Hofius and Harry enter at left—Hofius takes out handkerchief and wipes his eyes, then watches them soberly,

HOFIUS:—" Look at 'em, Harry; don't that look like a chromo? "

HARRY:—" Ladies, you are here early." [*Hofius and Harry go half way to top.*]

MABEL:—" We thought it would be pleasant here. How can I let Gertie leave me? Was that the boat whistle? "

HOFIUS:—" No. Don't get scart before you'r hurt." [*Snuffing.*]

GERTIE:—" Hofius, don't you let Mabel cry again, will you? "

HOFIUS:—" No, she shant, if I can help it." [*Nearly crying.*]
Enter Hilton R., stops at a distance, takes off hat.

HILTON:—" Gertrude. (*All turn to look at him.*) May God bless and protect you is the prayer of your uncle." [*Turns to go when she calls him, he returns.*]

GERTIE: —" Uncle, I have needed protection. I have prayed for it, and now I feel, in my heart, that my prayer is answered by rescuing me from the hands of my uncle. Farewell."

Waves hand—Hilton stands a few moments, then retreats at Right—Boat comes in—Mabel and Gertie embrace—Gertrude turns to go—Mabel kisses her again—Hofius and Harry go to bottom—Mabel weeping.

GERTIE:—" Do not weep, Mabel. Do anything but weep, I cannot bear tears."

HOFIUS:--[*Sobbing.*] " Mabel, can't you stop that crying? say! "

MABEL:—" I must cry. I cannot live without Gertie, I shall be so lonely." [*Hofius sits on grass and cries aloud.*]

HOFIUS:—" By gosh, that's more'n I can stand, and I haint nobody's calf neither." [*Gertie comes down rock and takes Hofius' hand.*]

GERTIE:—" Hofius, you should not care. I am not going many miles away."

HOFIUS:—" Don't make a tarnel bit of difference if you haint, for you know well enough we won't see you in a long time. You know you wont be here in a long time; you know you wont just as well as I do."

GERTIE:—[*Laughing.*] " Take good care of Mabel and write me sometimes. Good bye, Hofius. [*Shakes hands—Harry helps her on boat—She looks back and sees Mabel weeping.*) Dear Mabel, those tears are useless; it makes me feel terribly to see you weeping. (*Laughs.*) I would rather leave you laughing or singing. Let's sing our little mountain farewell. I would like to hear your voice last of all. Sing as long as you can hear me." [*BOTH SING.*]

CURTAIN.

ACT III. SCENE I. [Parlor.]

HOWARD :—[Seating herself in rocking-chair.] Well, I certainly have everything easy. I am born to luck. I have put in my time well since Gertie left; these long, weary months have not been very pleasant to Mabel. Yes, James Hilton believes in me and doubts his child. (Listening.) I hear voices; I presume it is Mabel and her father; they have a great many little jangles lately, since Gertie left. Yes, they are coming this way. I will know what it is about this time." [Conceals herself—Enter Hilton and Mabel.]

HILTON :—" Mabel, you have talked a long time and said nothing, substantially nothing. You press so hard on a subject that is no subject, that is purely immagination. I cannot be patient, I will not listen much longer."

MABEL :—" Oh, how very weak must be my lips, for God knows my heart is full. But oh, Papa, do listen to me if only for the love you bear me. If my words are senseless, do give me credit for the feeling that sends them forth. Kiss me and say you will listen."

'HILTON :—[Kisses Mabel.] " You are terribly excited, child; you act strange, very strange indeed " [Embraces her.]

MABEL :—" Yes, yes, I know it; I know that only too well."

HILTON :—" There, there; go on and say what you want to."

MABEL :—" Oh, how I dread to talk to you! I never thought I would fear to tell you any of my troubles, but I do, I do. Papa, you must not reproach me."

HILTON :—" My child, you are extremely sensative; I do not want to hurt your feelings. (Kisses her.) Go on."

MABEL :—" You remember last evening, when you were angry, you said that Harry Hanford was not an honorable young man. You wrong him. Papa. Had you told him to remain away from here he would have done so; but it was cruel to tell him that he was the means of seperating Ernest and I when he is so innocent."

HILTON :—" Is it to defend this Harry Hanford that you implore me to listen to you? Do you ask a boon of my love for his sake? Is this what you want? "

MABEL :—" No, no, Papa, no, no. Do be patient; I will soon reach the subject. Do not interrupt me. You have been deceived, made to believe that dear cousin Gertie was intriguing, that she seperated Ernest and I. Now, that she is away, you fall upon poor

Harry and say that it was he. Oh, I know why you think as you do. You are not yourself. No, that woman, that Mrs. Howard, has turned you. You are not the same kind, thoughtful father that you once were. Once you had sympathy for me, for all that was near you; but that woman, those eyes—"

HILTON:—" Mabel, I cannot hear you speak in such terms of Mrs. Howard; you wound me when you speak ill of her. I know what Gertrude Mason tried to do, but, through the kindness of Mrs. Howard, she failed to accomplish her purpose. Then Harry Hanford comes to take up the gauntlet where Gertie left off, but he, too, shall fail."

MABEL:—" How can she deceive you so? What can I say to make you see your error? I only hope you will know before it is too late. Do you believe all the bad things she tells you? "

HILTON:—" I believe all she tells me. She is a kind, sympathetic woman."

MABEL:—" She kind, she good, she, with those cruel eyes? Oh, Papa, for heaven's sake, are you mad? Yes, you must be. Did she not make you believe that I loved Ernest, and that Gertie and Harry came between us? "

HILTON:—" I know that it was impossible for any one to dislike Ernest; I know that Gertrude, in her selfishness, tried to win him, and, when she failed, she left Harry Hanford to finish. She told a falsehood to Loceno; that you have taken a considerable upon yourself, and that Harry Hanford was a nobody. These things I know."

MABEL:—" Such cruel things would never have entered your head had it not been for that woman. I will be truthful and tell you I despised Ernest Vaughn from the day I first saw him, but Harry Hanford I love with my whole heart."

HILTON:—" Mabel, this requires more patience than I possess; to to hear you speak in this way! Why, you lecture your father; you defend those who are your enemies; you speak unjustly of Mrs. Howard, a woman who would sacrifice her happiness for any little pleasure of yours. Ah, Mabel, could you have seen her weeping yesterday because of some careless and unthankful remark of yours, you would be ashamed of the manner in which you have spoken. There is some one filling your head with this trash and you are stupid to not see it."

MABEL:—" You talk very differently from the old way. I never heard anything but pet names from you until that woman came into our home. I have noticed the coldness creeping over you. Oh, Gertie, Harry and I must all be blamed because of that cruel woman."

HILTON:—" I will not hear your pleadings for Harry Hanford. I know why he comes here, but I forbid your seeing him; he must not come here again. You must not communicate in any way. Do you hear me? "

MABEL:—" I hear you. I hear you, but speak no more of him. (*Goes to him and takes hand.*) Much as I love Harry I will obey you. I can bear any sorrows for your sake, for Mamma's last words were· 'Love and obey your father.' Once we were happy in thinking and talking of her, Papa. Recall our home before she came here; we were so happy, so happy; but now you grow angry at me; scold me; you do not ask for kisses when you come to dinner; she takes my place at the table; you smile on her and reproach me, your child. I see it, every one sees it, and now, and now, my father, I ask you, for the sake of my dead mother, awake, awake, awake, Papa; you are asleep and the serpent is nestling in your bosom. Hear me, oh, hear me; I beg, I pray you from my soul."

HILTON:—" Mabel, do you believe, do you from your inmost heart, believe that Hester Howard is deceiving me? "

MABEL:—" I know she is; I know it, oh, so well."

HILTON:—" You think me a gray headed dolt; you think she controls me; you beg of me as if I were a maniac; you have shamefully wronged a noble woman; you have slandered her. I tell you she is a good woman and I intend to marry her, and the time is not far distant. Yes, I shall marry her if I live."

MABEL:—" Oh, God help me now! Retract those words or my heart will break. I would suffer anything for you; I would die for you; but I would rather see you dead than that woman's husband."

HILTON:—" I see plainly that you are beside yourself. (*Going to left.*) She will make you a good mother."

MABEL:—" Stop, father, it is a sacrilege."

HILTON:—[*Leaving.*] " I must leave you; I was a fool to remain so long." [*Exit L.*]

MABEL:—" Oh, my father! my father, God pity and forgive him. My once loving Papa; my once happy home; all gone! " [*Exit R.*]

HOWARD:—[*Entering from place of concealment.*] " That was indeed glorious. He has all confidence in me. Ah! I her mother! that was terrible for her to hear. Ha! ha! but I cannot help laughing. I her mother! ha! ha! haughty girl!. That was a bitter dose." [Exit R.]

NORA:—[*Entering with dusting rag.*] " Sometimes I wish I'd the money, then niver a bit o' throuble wud I have. I'd have me Bridget, I'd have me Nora and I'd have me housekeeper wid Tim as the master. Ah, yis, Tim as the Mr. Finnegan and I the Mrs. Finnegan. Yit, money don't buy happiness, it can't buy happiness, no, now ye'r talkin' ; it don't buy happiness. Didn't I meet Miss Mabel a cryin' an' a cryin' as though her little heart wud break? The foinest little girrul in the land. (*Crying.*) Yis, now that I am started a cryin' I may jist as well do it all at wunst and shed a few beautiful tears for Tim, for Tim, the brave. (*Takes letter from pocket.*) Guess I will read yer letther again. Tim, if ye don't moind, I can't make out this writin', but I can remember what Mabel said was in here, so I will jist rade it to meself this toime. (*Snuffing and crying.*] " Me own darlint Nora, me own darlint Nora. I am nearly crazy wid grief, a grievin' for me Nora." (*To audience.*) Ah, that sounds like Tim; he! he! (*Thinking.*) Now, yhat was it he said next; what was it. Ah, yis, I have it now, " The days are so long, and so long widout me Nora. Niver a noight do I shlape for the dreamin' o' me Nora." Now, what was the nixt he wroted? it was the swatest of all, but, bother me life, I can't remimber it. It was swater thin anything yez ever heard." [*Enter Hofius, frightens Nora.*]

HOFIUS:—" Say, Nora, reading your love letter? "

NORA:—" I was readin' a letther, a short letther from me mither in ould Oireland."

HOFIUS:—" Does she write a ' swate ' letter? [*Enter Mabel dressed for a walk. To Mabel.*] Nora was just perusing a short letter from her mother."

MABEL:—" What do you mean, Hof., Nora has no mother."

NORA:—[*Leaving.*] " Now, Miss Mabel, you have ixposed me. I don't care, he was very insultin' to me, an' I wud loike to see the girrul that wud be afther ownin' it. I'd lie, mesilf, afore I'd say it was Tim; sure I wud."   [Exit back.]

MABEL:—" You and Nora do not seem to be the best of friends, do you? I am going for a short walk, am in hopes of feeling better on my return."

HOFIUS:—" Mabel, I hate to see you look so blue, you look so awful down the mouth. I guess I'll go home. I haven't saw you act good since Gertie left. Oh, I suppose you are getting tired of me."

MABEL:—" Why, Coz., you must not talk this way; I do not know what I should do if you were to leave me. I will feel better from being out in the air awhile. No matter what is said or done you must not go away, as you are the only one in the house that cares for me."

HOFIUS:--" You are darned right I care for you. I should say I did care for you. Gosh all fire-bugs! you bet I care for you."

MABEL:--" We are cousins and have the privilege of liking each other, but it would be ridiculous should we think of falling in love."

HOFIUS;—[*Looks surprised.*] " It would? "

MABEL:--" Why, certainly! But, of course, you and I do not want to. I must go; good bye, Coz." [Exit L.]

HOFIUS:—" That's the way it is, is it? We don't want to fall in love, eh. Well, may be we don't, and then, agin, may be we do. Why, I'm too fur gone this minnit to say *I* don't want to. I'm right there. No, by thunder, I'm right there. By gosh, I do love her, and I kind a think she does me, but she is bashful like all girls." [*Opens book. Enter Mrs. Howard.*]

HOWARD:—" Why, Hofius, I thought your cousin, Mabel, was with you."

HOFIUS:—" She was, but [*Looking solemn.*] she felt so tarnel downhearted she went out walkin'. (*Enter Nora with duster.*) Say, Nora, (*Laughing.*) got any more love letters from your mother? " [*Nora acts angry.*]

HOWARD: –" Poor Mabel, I know she is far from well. Her father and I think it would be pleasant for her to go down in the country with you when you go home."

HOFIUS:--[*Looks surprised.*] Who said I was going home? I didn't know that I was. If Mabel wants me to I will, but as she does not I think I'll stay here a year or two."

NORA:—" Ah, yis, I think milkin' the cows and feeding the pigs is better fur the loikes o' ye thin preachin' from that book from mornin' 'till noight."

HOFIUS:—[*Surprised.*] " Oh! oh! you don't say so! Well, Nora, your mother writes a good hand for a dead woman."

HOWARD:—" Do you know which way Mabel went? She seems so miserable lately I realy feel uneasy." [Exit L.]

HOFIUS:—" That woman is enough to set a feller crazy."

NORA:—" Faith, an' I thought yis was that alridy."

HOFIUS:—" May be I am, but I can tell a live letter from a dead one." [Exit L.]

NORA:—" Good riddance to bad rubbish." [Exit.]

SCENE II.

Park—Enter Mabel walking slowly—Sits on rustic seat—Looks up at birds—
    Birds sing.

MABEL:—" Oh, birdie, you sing as though you were happy. How
sweetly you sing, how happy. Sing on; I, too, was once happy;
not a care; my home was as free for me as the great tree is for you.
(*Bird sings.*) Sing on, sing on; it brings the memory of my
mother's loving face and my fathers (*Mrs. Howard enters and
conceals herself.*) gentle voice. Oh, Papa! if you knew my heart,
I am as innocent as the little bird that sings so happily. Oh, Merciful Heavens, where is my home? Peace, happiness, love of home
are strangers to me. Is it possible this is the happy, lighthearted
Mabel Hilton? No! no! I cannot believe it! (*Harry appears and
watches Mabel unnoticed.*) Oh, my Papa, why do you drive me
from your heart? I have none but you! (*Clasps hands.*) Merciful Father, sustain me. Thou who hast watched in my happiness,
give me strength to endure this misery. Lord, in mercy, hear my
prayer! "

HARRY:—[*Approaching her.*] " Mabel, how came you here? "
[*Takes both hands.*]

MABEL:—" Why, Harry, I did not think of seeing you here or I
should not have come. Do, do not hold my hands. I did not
think of seeing you."

HARRY:—" Mabel, are you so sorry to find me here? Have you
been taught to hate me? Is my presence unbearable? "

MABEL:—" No, no, Harry, but Papa told me I should never speak
to you again; I promised him I would not; he would be angry if he
knew I was here with you; yet, he should forgive when he knows
the meeting was not premeditated."

HARRY:—" He would not blame you, we did not suspect seeing
each other. Dear Mabel, I cannot remain away from you much
longer." [*Draws her toward him.*]

MABEL:—" 'Tis so sweet to be near you, Harry. Such happiness
cannot be wrong, but I told Papa I would not and I cannot stay
here."

HARRY:—" How long must this continue? Promise me, Mabel,
that in one year, if you are still so unhappy, you will come with me,
let circumstances be what they may."

MABEL:—" No, I cannot promise that. I am needed at home,
Papa will think differently some time, then he will not blame you."

HARRY:—" Then you refuse to promise me even though I wait a year? Ah, Mabel, I cannot believe you love me. Had I thousands at my command, a beautiful home to take you to, I think then you might promise me; but I have not. This, I fear, is why you hesitate."

MABEL:—" Harry, it is cruel for you to talk to me in this manner, it is so far from my thoughts. You are ambitious, truthful, trusting; you are all I would care to have you. Supposing you cannot indulge in all the luxuries at present, am I so lost to sense and honor that a few paltry dollars would make me care less for you? You do not understand me. To do for yourself is to know yourself; you are better for it; it helps to bring out all that is noble and good. I must remain in my home and you can only trust me."

HARRY:—" I will trust you, Mabel, but I sincerely hope I shall not be obliged to wait too long. Is there anything I can do to help you? "

MABEL:—" No, nothing. (*Appears frightened.*) I must return or someone may see me. Oh, Harry, I do not know when I shall see you again. I promised Papa I would not see you or write you. Do not look so*downcast, this must end soon some way; things cannot go on this way forever."

HARRY:—" I presume you must go, yet we have been here a very short time."

MABEL:—" Yes, and were we to stay all day it would be a short time to us. So, Harry, cheer up, we will soon be happy; we cannot endure so much without some reward in the future. I must go."

HARRY:—" You will be true to me I know, but before you leave me let me put Love's ancient seal upon the pledge."

Kisses her—Mabel exits right—Harry watches her until out of sight, then dons hat and exits slowly at left.

SCENE III.

Path through woods—Enter Hofius at left, book in hand, hat on back of head.

HOFIUS:—" I can't think where Mabel can be such a long time. I'll bet I'll go along next time. Sometimes I wish I had never come here; I should have thought a dum sight more of uncle Jim and not half so much of Mabel. She is sometimes as sweet as pie, then, again, she's a spunky little rat. I don't suppose she's anywhere singing sweet songs of me."   [Exit L.]

SCENE IV.

Parlor—Enter Mrs. Howard.

HOWARD:—" No, Mabel isn't here yet. I shall mention the fact to her father. I will tell him I saw them together. She cannot deny meeting him. Ah, my victory is well nigh complete. (*Enter Mabel*) Why, Mabel, I was fretting about you; I feared something had happened you. [*Mabel throws hat on sofa.*]

MABEL:—" Fretting about me? I presume you fretted for fear something would *not* happen me. I do not care to listen to any more of your deceitfulness and I wish to be alone."

Enter Hilton and Vaughn—Mrs. Howard turns to go, when Hilton addresses her—Mabel shakes hands with Vaughn, seems delighted to see him.

HILTON:—" Mrs. Howard, this is my old friend, Charles Vaughn."

HOWARD:—[*Turning her head as if to conceal her face.*] I am pleased to meet you, sir."

VAUGHN:—" Why, Hester Davidson, I am indeed surprised to see you here among my friends."

HOWARD:—" You are undoubtedly mistaken, sir, as I do not remember of ever meeting you."

VAUGHN:—" No, oh no! I am not mistaken, I know you, oh, so well. Ha! ha! What new name have you now? Where is your brother-in-law and niece? I know where they are, they are starving and you spending their money."

HOWARD: —" I tell you, sir, I am not that person. James, Mr. Hilton, I cannot endure this; such insolence, such falsehoods! " [*Puts handkerchief to face and weeps bitterly.*]

MABEL:—" Mr. Vaughn, are you sure you know her? "

VAUGHN:—" Know her? yes indeed, Mabel. I have known her for ten years, but I never expected to see her here until I saw her brother-in-law to-day. She will ruin the household if she remains here."

MABEL:—" Thank God! Then, perhaps, my father is saved."

HILTON:—" Charles Vaughn is mistaken. I know he is, for this lady is not such a woman."

HOWARD:—" How I am wronged! (*Weeping.*) Is there no one to defend me? "

VAUGHN:—" No one that knows you would defend you."

HILTON:—" Charles Vaughn, you have always been my friend and now do not continue to pour out insults on an innocent woman that I have sworn to protect." [*Mrs. Howard sobs aloud.*]

VAUGHN:—" I am only glad that you are not married as I can convince you in less than an hour that I am not mistaken. You are not the only one that has been deceived by her."

MABEL:—" Then, Mr. Vaughn, for my sake, spare no pains in making him see it. Then I can again have a happy home."

HILTON:—" Silence, Mabel! You are too willing to believe anything against her." [*Enter Hofius, notices quarrel, goes to Mabel frightened.*]

HOWARD:—" Must I endure this? (*To Vaughn.*) No matter how strong may be the resemblance to some guilty person. I am innocent of anything wrong, and dear Mr. Hilton, I must be protected." [*Sobbing.*]

HILTON:—" I regret to say that you are rather impertinent, and further, sir, that your statements are ridiculous."

MABEL:—" Oh, Papa, let him proceed. Mr. Vaughn, make him know her as I know her."

HOWARD:—" Dear, dear! and your child believes all! how can I endure so much from her whom I love so dearly! "

HOFIUS:—" Yes you do, just about as well as— "

HILTON:—" We will manage this without any assistance from you, sir."

HOFIUS:—" Yes, I suppose you can, but you know I never liked that darned woman since she got Gertie in that awful scrape. (*aside*) There, I've said it anyhow." [*Sits.*]

VAUGHN:—" Well, James, I will go back to the hotel; when I again see you you may feel differently. I would not wound your feelings, but I will not stay near you and see you deceived, so good day."

HILTON:—[*Coldly.*] Good day. (*Exit Vaughn L.*) My dear Hesther, do not feel so badly, I know he is mistaken and he shall never trouble me any more; this is his last visit in my home."

MABEL:—" But, Papa, she did not deny, emphatically, that her name was Davidson." [*Mrs. Howard sobs anew.*]

HILTON:—" Mabel, your actions have been singular in connection with this affair, you even rebuked me for saying I would defend her from insolence, from stories so untrue."

MABEL:—" I beg pardon, but she did not show innocence by standing up and denying the charge, or asking him to prove it."

HILTON:—" What! do you mean to say that you credit the infamous story? Charles Vaughn would not lie, he is mistaken in the person; the statement was ridiculous, extremely ridiculous. and you credit it."

MABEL:—" I said nothing of the kind, I merely stated that she expressed an hysterical astonishment but did not flatly contradict the assertion."

HOWARD:—" Do you imagine, my dear, that I would tell Mr. Vaughn he lied, merely because he had the audacity to throw those words in my face? "

MABEL:—" I only want her to say yes, or no."

HILTON:—" Mabel, I cannot, for the life of me, imagine the cause of your acting so unnaturally; will you tell me? Perhaps you are ill, I never thought of that. Is it so, my child? "

MABEL:—" No, Papa, I only want her to say yes, or no."

HILTON:—" Mabel, you are wilful and obstinate."

HOWARD:—[*Rocking and crying hysterically.*] " I see how it is, I see it all. Oh, dear! oh, dear! Mabel thinks I am a li-li-liar! (*Hilton tries to soothe her. Hofius laughs to himself.*) Oh, dear! how can she hate me so when I love her so much! I am sorry I came here; don't talk to me, James, I am going to leave your house." [*Rises.*]

HILTON: —" No, no; you shall do no such thing; take some of this wine." [*Gives her wine which she drinks eagerly.*]

HOFIUS:—[*Aside.*] " She seems to have a pretty good mouth for that, too."

HILTON:—" Now you will feel better."

HOWARD:—" You are so kind, but oh. I cannot stay here. If Mabel thinks I am a liar, no, no, I will go. (*Hilton catches her arm and seats her.*) She don't love me, she disbelieves me."

HILTON:—" Let me get you some more wine, dear Hesther. Remain here until I return." [*Exit L. for wine.*]

HOFIUS:—[*Mrs. Howard rocking and crying.*] " Say, old woman, keep right on crying and rocking; if the chair can stand it we can."

HOWARD: —" Oh, I will go this very night to the hotel." [*Enter Hilton.*]

HILTON:—" No, no; you shall do no such thing. Take this wine. My daughter's unguarded words shall not drive you from me."

HOWARD:—" But you will not be happy if I stay. I could not remain if there was one it the house that did not like me. But oh, when I think of leaving you it tears my very heart strings. You who have been so kind to me; but I cannot stay, I must go." [rises]

HILTON:—" You must not. I cannot spare you, you shall remain."

HOWARD:—" No, let me go. Oh, dear, oh heavens, I shall go mad; to call me Mrs. Davidson! oh, how cruel, how cruel! I will go."

HILTON:—" You see, Mabel, what you have done. but she shall not suffer." [Hilton and Mrs. Howard exit L.]

HOFIUS:—" I guess the old man will git his eye peeled by the time Mr. Vaughn gets here."

MABEL:—" How can Papa be so blinded. She had a terrible spell; (Laughs.) that was a regular old tantrum wasn't it. Coz.? I do really believe that Papa is going to find her out; oh, how I hope he is." [Both exit.]

SCENE V.

Path, same as in SCENE III—Harry enters slowly.

HARRY:—" The old family grove. We are often superstitious; I fancied that if I came here just at this particular moment I might see one I knew; that I might see Mabel. I felt so confident she would be here. It seems so long since I saw her face; I fear something is wrong. I may as well return, I shall not see her; no. no." [Sighs and returns. Enter Mabel slowly.]

MABEL:—" No, no one here! How lonely it looks. I thought some one would happen here if I came now; no one here; I am dissapointed. But I may have been too late. Last night, in my dreams, I saw my mother. This was once as sacred a day for my father as it now is for me. Every year since my mother's death my father and I have always held this day and night in memory by talking of her and singing her favorite songs; but what will he do tonight? He treats me so cruely of late I fear to go to his library; if he is there I shall begin to think he still loves me. Perhaps he is somewhat surprised at Mr. Vaughn's words. Oh, if he can ever know, then I will be happy again. (Grows dark.) But my mother said: 'Go to your father and I will be there.' Yes, I will go, it is getting late and oh! a storm is arising! If it should storm as it did the night my mother died, and Papa not let me go to his room, oh, that would be more than I could bear. O! what a storm! how I dread to start!" [Exit L.]

SCENE VI.

Library—Dark night—Small light—Wind gradually raising.

HILTON: —[*Enters.*] " I wonder if Mabel has been here and not
seeing me, gone. No, no; she has forgotten this night, or she may
be afraid to come to me. (*Goes to window.*) What a dark night,
and it grows darker. (*Thunders.*) What thunder! oh, what a terrible night. I alone; how my solitude oppresses me. Five years ago
to-night, Martha, my wife, died and left me alone with little Mabel;
just such a dark, stormy night. Mabel and I have ever held this
sacred; but Mabel is not the same child she was a year ago; (*Lightning.*) but oh, how I wish she would come. There are times when
it is terrible to be alone and old. At any other time I could seek
the society of Mrs. Howard and be happy; but not to-night. This
night belongs to Martha, Mabel and myself. (*Lightnings.*) How
the blue lightning skims along the surface and seems to set all on
fire. Yes, I feel lonely. not because of any vain hunger for past
enjoyment never to be known again; but the memories. There is
no place in the universe where one can go to banish from within
the eyelids. the dear dead faces, or from the heart that throbs no
longer any passions of its own. (*Thunders.*) 'Tis terrible to be
alone; I shall send for Mabel. (*knock at door.*) Can it be Mabel?
none other can enter here. (*Sitting. Calls.*) Mabel! "

MABEL:—" Yes, Papa." [*Hilton opens door, kisses her on entering.*]

HILTON:—" Ah, my child. I feared you had forgotten."

MABEL:—[*Sits on stool at his feet. Both sit.*] " Forgotten. Papa!
I could not forget, but I feared you had."

HILTON:—" Come what may, this night shall ever be held sacred
to the memory of your mother. I had such a dream last night; it
seemed it was for the purpose of reminding me of to-night; but
God knows I would not forget it."

MABEL:—" Papa, I, too, had a dream; 'twas so strange and yet so
real; had it not been for that dream I should never ventured in here
to-night. (*Thunders.*) May I tell it to you? "

HILTON:—" Yes, go on, dear."

MABEL:—" When I was nearly asleep I had the feeling of one
floating, then I became still and Mamma came to me; so beautiful,
oh, so beautiful, Papa. She said: " Dear Mabel. go to your Papa's
room to-morrow night; he will let you in; be kind to him, he loves
you." Then I asked: " Mamma, are you sure Papa loves me? "
and her face seemed to light up so beautifully as she answered:

" Loves you? ah, child, since my death he has known no other love but yours. There may be a strange fancy, a strange something you cannot fathom, but that, Mabel, will soon be over." She looked so beautiful, so sad and said: "You shall not suffer long for I am watching over you both." I could feel the kisses, the same sweet kisses, the loving caresses I have learned to live without. Then she asked me to sing the little song I used to sing, and, Papa, it seemed as though I, too, was an angel for the moment. I commenced to sing and such strange, sweet music accompanied me; I felt that I could sing forever there. 'Twas a beautiful sight to see; she so lovely, telling me to be kind to you, and that some day, and soon, too, all difficulties would be removed. Are you listening, Papa? "

HILTON :—" Yes. yes; go on, dear. I sometimes feel that the spirits of our loved ones do return."

MABEL :—" She implored me to tell you that a great revelation is soon to come to you and that you must accept it. She kissed me again and again, then passed away. (*Thunders and showers.*) Oh, what a terrible night! how the rain splashes against the pane, and the blue lightning skims o'er the surface; 'tis a terrible night! But I feel weary and must retire."

HILTON :—" Yes, 'tis late and you are weary, but can you not sing the song for me as you did for your mother? "

MABEL :—" Oh. I am not too weary to sing if you wish me to. (*Takes up guitar and sings. Song ended, sets it down.*) Good night, Papa; (*Kisses him.*) good night."

HILTON : —" Good night, darling, good night."

Exit Mabel, left—Hilton remains sometime as if in thought, then Exits left.

SCENE VII.

Parlor as as in SCENE IV—Mrs. Howard seated in rocking chair.

HOWARD :—" To-morrow ends all trouble, for James Hilton and I shall then be one. Ah, if Miss Mabel knew what the morrow will bring forth she would not be so happy to-day. James Hilton would condemn all for me: his daughter, his friends. all for me. Should Charles Vaughn ever convince him of the truth it will be when we are married, and then he cannot get away. How I long for the morrow; happy as I try to be, I feel that there is a dark cloud hovering o'er me. Ah, should the truth come out where would I be? Hester Davidson. indeed! Again friendless and alone. But I must not harbor such thoughts. (*Hears footsteps.*) Someone is coming; I hope it is James." [*Enter Hofius.*[

HOFIUS:—[*Bowing.*] " Ah! oh! 'tis you, Mrs. Davidson, Howard, I mean. I thought you had gone back on the Hilton mansion the way you dug out of here last night, but it seems that you and the old rocking-chair are here again. Yes; oh, I was sure you had skipped."

HOWARD:—" I intended going but your uncle would not listen to it. You may be surprised when you ascertain who is to go. I am more at home here than you imagine." [*Enter Mabel with hat and wraps. Postman rings.*]

MABEL:—" Come, Coz., let's go to the landing; there's going to be a boat race." [*Enter Hilton with paper,*]

NORA:—[*Entering with letter.*] " A letther for Miss Mabel." [*Mabel reads address.*]

MABEL:—" 'Mr. James Hilton or Miss Mabel.' (*Hilton listens. Mabel opens letter.*) " Mr. Hilton and daughter come immediately to 384 Rush St., up two flights of stairs, and you will learn something to your advantage both socially and financially, (*Exit Howard*) Do not delay, come immediately. YOUR FRIEND, ———" I cannot read the initials. What do you think of it, shall we go? "

HILTON:—" Something to our advantage *financially*! certainly we will go. I will tell Mrs. Howard that I am called away, and see that she wants for nothing. Put on your wraps. (*Retires a short time, then returns with hat cane, etc.*) Hofius, should Hesther need any assistance that Nora cannot render, you see to it. She is far from being well, and I cannot find her."

HOFIUS:—[*Aside*] " Yes, I'd like to 'tend to her once, sometime, for instance, when she gets them cantankerous bighpoles."

MABEL:—" So would I. (*Laughs. Hilton exit L. Mabel follows.*) Good bye, Coz." [*Throws kiss.*]

HOFIUS:—" Darn that girl, she threw that kiss just as careless as could be, and I felt it clean to my toes quicker'n lightning. Pshaw! what should I care for her. There's Sue Wright, bless her little heart, I spose if I went home I'd have to marry her. I don't care to marry just now, I want to flirt around awhile longer. But I spose I'd have to marry her if I went home or hear something about that blasted old cow or pig, and by thunder I wont pay no twenty-five dollars to none of the widder Wrightsesses." [*Enter Nora.*]

NORA:—" **Mr.** Haskins, will you please, sir, if you please, go into the room and help Mrs. Howard? she's nearly wild wid pain." [**Exit** right.]

HOFIUS:—" You bet I'll help. Now for some fun." [Exit R.]

SCENE VIII.

Harold's room—Harold on lounge—Minnie on Vaughn's lap.

HAROLD:—" Do you believe they will come? I am growing worse." [*Minnie goes to him.*]

VAUGHN:—" Yes, I am sure he will; if he does not soon come I will go and bring him." [*Knock at door, Vaughn opens, Enter Mabel and Hilton.*]

HILTON:—[*Surprised.*] " You here, Charles? is it you who wanted me? "

VAUGHN:—" Yes; a little longer and you would have been too late. I have known this man, who lies dying here, for the last three years. I have not seen him, did not know his whereabouts until I saw his little daughter on the street yesterday. Now, Harold, tell him what you have to say."

HAROLD:—" I feel very weak, bring me some wine. (*Minnie goes for wine.*) I was once surrounded with every luxury; a kind and loving wife, (*Minnie gives wine.*) everything to make me happy. During my days of plenty my wife's sister shared our home. When Elsie, my wife, died, and my eyesight failed me, I became helpless; one misfortune followed another until—until my little Minnie has led her father around a blind, blind beggar. (*He lays back on pillow, Minnie caressing him.*) There was a terrible crime committed sometime ago and an enemy threw it upon me; every chance was against me, all believed me guilty, so I fled for my life as I knew my little daughter needed me. I know I am blind, but I am her father. This sister knew the whole circumstance; knew I was innocent, but she kept the money, telling me that if I made any attempt to recover what belonged to me she would advise them of my whereabouts; she has threatened me many times. My wife was a lovely woman, but her sister has been more cruel than I ever dreamed a human being could be. She has laughed at our cries for food. More wine, Minnie. Laughed at our hunger, but she cannot laugh long; no, no. Minnie will have a home when I am gone; Mr. Vaughn will give her a home."

MINNIE:—" Oh, Papa, I am going with you."

HAROLD:—" Now, Mr. Hilton, this sister-in-law has been the originator of many disturbances in families; her name is Hesther Davidson, she goes by the name of Howard. Get her out of your house or you will rue it."

HILTON:—" What, sir! you do not mean to say that this woman, this wicked woman you speak of, is my housekeeper? "

HAROLD:—" Yes, the same, the very same."

HILTON:—" You do not know what you say; you are led into this by her enemy, Charles Vaughn."

HAROLD:—" Minnie, show him the picture of your aunt Hesther and her last husband. I have been to your house for food and she would have turned me away hungry had it not been for your daughter; perhaps she remembers when Minnie fainted at the door, and Hesther called us beggars."

MABEL:—" Yes, indeed, I do." [*Minnie shows picture.*]

HILTON:—" Oh, heaven! can this be true? This *is* her face. Can it be that I have been so blind to all? "

HAROLD: —[*Rising partially.*] " I feel weaker; I am going fast. I could not die without your knowing this. 'Tis true and may God help all who depend on *her* mercy. Oh, Minnie! "

HILTON:—" Can it be true? " [*Minnie weeps.*]

HAROLD:—" Oh, Minnie, do not grieve, you will have a home and I will no longer be in your way."

MINNIE:—" Oh, Papa, let me go with you, I can't stay here alone."

MABEL:—" Papa, I want Minnie with us; she would not be so lonely, and I have no one with me. Don't you want her to? "

HILTON:—" Certainly I do if her father and Mr. Vaughn will consent. Minnie shall never be troubled by the housekeeper, as one so wicked as she cannot find shelter in my home."

HAROLD:—" Then take her, I know you will be kind to her. You will be happy, darling, in your new home, (*Soft music.*) and I shall be happy in mine. Oh, heaven, so, *so* beautiful! "

MINNIE: —" Oh, Papa, I want to go with. I must go with you, I cannot stay here with no Papa to kiss me, no Papa to love me."

HAROLD:—" Minnie, my child, don't cry so, they will love you, they will care for you, and you will no longer be a little beggar, never again be hungry."

MINNIE:—" Yes, I know I have been hungry sometimes, but I was always happy with you, you loved me. Oh, Papa, no one will ever love me as you do; do not die and leave me."

MABEL:—" Do not fear, Minnie, we will love and care for you."

HAROLD:—" Yes, I know you will care for her, God bless you for it. 'T is good that I can die, then Minnie will no longer suffer. In heaven your mother awaits me."

MINNIE:—" Oh, Papa, let me go with you to Mamma, she loves me; don't leave me, take me with you to Mamma. Oh, how pale you are, shall I get some wine? Papa, why don't you answer me? (To Vaughn.) Why don't Papa talk to me, is he asleep."

VAUGHN:—" Dear child, your father is dying."

MINNIE:—" Oh, no, no; wait a little longer. Oh, dear Papa, you must not die, you must not die."

VAUGHN:—[Placing hand on Harold's head.] " Yes, he is dead."

MINNIE:—" Dead? my Papa dead? He is not dead, he is blind, that is why his eyes are shut. No, Papa cannot die. (Takes hand.) Oh, Papa, your hands are so cold, so cold! (Kisses him.) Your face is so cold! Can't you talk, Papa? can't you talk to me? He does not smile on his little Minnie. Don't you know my kisses? Won't he ever kiss me again, never kiss me? Papa, darling, are you dead? dead? Yes; I know he is dead!" [Falls across her father's body—Tableau---Tableau lights--Angel decends.]

CURTAIN.

ACT IV. SCENE I.

Parlor—Hilton reading—Hofius studying and making gestures—Minnie sitting
on stool near Mabel, learning crocheting.

MABEL:—" Here, Minnie; cross the stitches and then knit back
three."

HILTON:—" What are you learning, Minnie? making a fishing
net? "

MINNIE:—" No, sir. Who ever heard of making a fish net with a
crochet needle? I am making a tidy for your easy chair in the
library."

MABEL:—" Minnie, have you seen Gertie? I wonder if she has
given up her ride? I thought she went to dress a long time ago."

HOFIUS:—" Say, Uncle Jim., did you ever see that horse that
Gertie rides? Why, that Dexter is the firiest horse in the
whole city! but she won't have any other, and she'll break her
neck some day, just you see if she don't. But then, she haint no
more like herself than a dove is like a catamount. If she had stayed
another year at that school she'd had to have an introduction to
herself." [Enter Gertie in riding-habit, whip in hand.]

GERTIE:—" Hofius, is Dexter ready? "

HOFIUS:—" I dunno, but I can go and see. I should think you'd
be scared to death riding that horse; he'll kill you yet."

GERTIE:—[Laughing.] " No, Hofius, Dexter knows me. (Exit
Hofius.) Mabel. put on your gloves and come with me. Uncle,
do you not think she ought to accompany me? I dislike to go
alone, and shall race if she does not."

HILTON:—" Certainly, Mabel, you should. Your pony needs exercise."

MABEL:—" I cannot, Papa, as Ernest Vaughn is at the hotel and
I expect him any moment. [Gertie seems agitated.]

GERTIE:—" Ernest Vaughn! Ernest here in the city again, is
he? Perhaps I may see him; but he, I presume, would scarcely
recognize me; I do not look so young as I did. (Aside.) Ah, Mabel,
my time is coming; Ernest Vaughn shall know me. (Looks out of
window.) Here is Dexter. now. (Enter Hofius.) Au revoir! " [Waves

hand, exit L. followed by Hilton.]

MINNIE:—" Is she not beautiful? "

MABEL:—" Yes, indeed."

HOFIUS:—" Isn't she crazy, I should say; crazy as a bed bug. What does ail Gertrude, any way? Why, Mabel do you know I am perfectly shamed to think I ever loved that girl as I did? I guess if we knew the whole truth of the matter she didn't go to any school down the river, but jined a circus. Lord! she haint afeered o' nothin', so she haint. Why, she can beat anybody I ever see ride. (*Minnie exit L.*) I haven't saw anything to match her."

MABEL:—" This is all very funny for you. So you loved *her* did you? and Sue Wright and I, too. Ah, Coz., you are a little too fickle."

HOFIUS:—" Sposin' I did love you, what good did it do me? Don't you spose I know that Harry Hanford is your sweetness? Course you think I am as green as a summer squash, but, Mabel, you won't think I am so green and so fickle when I tell you that I am going to stick to Sue Wright. Mrs. Howard haint here to tell me to go home, but I can go, just the same. I had a great long, long letter from Sue, last night, just chuck full o' sweet things, briming over with sweet words. Sue has gone into the milliner business, sold her share in the farm. Yes, she is going to trim hats and bonnets for all Squash Holler. Her shop is right down town where you can see everybody. They want me to go home and they will have a shin-dig for me; get up a big dance, they say. It haint any polite party or hop, as you call 'em. I am going to play the fiddle myself. I begin to hanker arter a good, old fashiond break-down. Darn it, Mabel, you ought to go to one real good dance; a dance where the folks git up and crack the tune down. We didn't happen to have any when you were down there." [*Enter Nora with card to Mabel. Reads.]*

MABEL:—" Ernest Vaughn. Show him in, Nora. Now, Hofius, I do not want you to mention Gertie's name in any way, no matter what is said; I do not want him to know she is here, unless he may ask. (*Enter Ernest. Mabel rises.*) Mr. Vaughn, I am indeed pleased to see you." [*Shake hands.]*

ERNEST:—" Thanks; I owe one summer's happiness to this home."

MABEL:—" Mr. Vaughn, this is my cousin, Mr. Haskins, perhaps you have forgotten him." [*Shake hands.]*

HOFIUS:—" You left here that summer a few days after I got here, but I remember you well, and if I didn't I'd feel pretty well ac-quainted, hearing the girls talk of you so much." [*Mabel scowls.]*

ERNEST:--" My natural curiosity leads me to enquire who these young ladies may be? "

HOFIUS:--[*Aside.*] " I've stepped in it! [*Turns head gently.*] Why, you see, Mrs. Howard, what used to do the house-keepin' here, she turned out to be a fraud and Uncle Jim just naturally shipped her. And he took a little girl to raise, to do by her as they would by their own child. I didn't hear them say much about you, only that you were in town; Mabel was telling her, you know. [*Aside.*] I'm out of that."

ERNEST:--" I saw a young lady riding a horse that looked very much like Dexter; she rode beautifully and managed her horse perfectly; none but an experienced equestrian could do so well."

HOFIUS:--" I know who it is, don't you, Mabel? " [*Mabel scowls*]

ERNEST:--" Is it a lady of my acquaintance? her countenance looked familiar."

HOFIUS:--" No, no; we don't know for sure, but I thought if I could have saw her I might have told, for we know most everybody 'round these diggens." [*Enter Gertie L., does not notice Ernest. Takes off gloves.*] •

GERTIE:--" Dear Mabel, I have enjoyed myself so much; Dexter was full of life to-day. (*Observes Ernest.*) Ah! excuse me! I was not aware of strangers." [*Bows low.*].

MABEL:--" Mr. Vaughn, my cousin, Gertie; do you not remember her? "

ERNEST:--" Yes, indeed, I remember her. I scarcely dared hope for the pleasure of meeting you again. I do not think I should have known you had we met in another place."

GERTIE:--" Indeed! have I changed so much? I had not forgotten your face, but perhaps my memory is better than others."

ERNEST:--" One can change very much in three years, Miss Mason, but I remember the pleasant summer I passed here; that requires no great taxation of the memory."

GERTIE:--" I assure you I have not forgotten. (*To Mabel.*) I must tease you a little, Mabel. Harry was at the corners with his pony, and we raced to the landing; on our arrival we found a number of young people boating. We had several races; the river was beautiful; every one of us became perfectly desperate in our anxiety to excel." [*Enter Harry.*]

HARRY:--" Excuse me for entering so uncerimoniously, but Nora informed me there were no strangers present. Mabel, why did you remain at home? I tried to persuade Ernest to go but he refused me point blanc. Ah, Gertie, they are the loosers. Gertie, the prize was awarded to you, saying you had no equal in rowing."

GERTIE:—" Thanks; it was a great pleasure to me."

HARRY:—" Ernest, come with me to the office, the ladies will weary of you if you remain too long. I want you the rest of the day, beside, I must make arrangements for the party."

ERNEST: -[*Rising.*] "I do not imagine the young ladies will mourn my absence to any great extent as I have been uncommonly stupid. Yes, I will go anywhere, anywhere out in the world. (*To Gertie.*) I presume we will meet again at the party?" [*Gertie bows assent. Exit Ernest and Harry L., Gertie R. Harry whispers to Mabel.*]

HOFIUS:—[*Angrily.*] "That looks like manners to whisper in company. don't it? These city folks think they are just old manners itself; but if I had whispered in company my dad would have threshed me quicker'n you could say Jack Robinson. (*Mabel laughs*) Why don't he say a dance; that's just what it is. I don't want to go, but it's nothing more or less than a dance."

MABEL:—" Why are you so cross. Hofius?"

HOFIUS:—" Nothin' in particular. They didn't say a word about my going to the dance. did they? I haint a going either; I don't want to go, but if I did go I would put on my good clothes; I've got 'em and you know it. I'd go and set in the corner and laugh at 'em. Such dancing! (*Takes coat tail in each hand and imitates modern waltzing.*) That's all there is of it."

MABEL:—[*Laughing.*] " Why, Cousin, no one ever looked so bad as that."

HOFIUS: --" Yes. they do. but you wont own it. You slide 'round the same way."

MABEL:—" Hofius, how cross and hateful you are. I thought you were getting real good, but I declare, you are meaner than ever."

HOFIUS:—" To tell the truth, Miss Hilton, I think I have stayed here about long enough, don't think I am needed since Gertie came back, and Harry Hanford is snoopin' around here more than half the time; then. next comes that lazy, shiftless, sneaking Vaughn."

MABEL:—" How mean you talk. I know you have been very kind to me, I do not know what I should have done in the last three years had it not been for you."

HOFIUS:—" That's it exactly. Haint I stuck by you like a tick.

through thick and thin? if I haint, Hofius Thaddeus Haskins don't know what the word means, but then I am going down where Sue is; we'll have a dance down there that *is* a dance, and I'll fiddle, too. I am going to pack up my satchel and dig right out. Tell Gertie good bye for me. (*Walks to and fro, watching the effect of his leaving on Mabel.*) I'll gather up my elocution books and skip. May be I'll give a reading when down there, they don't hear fine readers every day."

MABEL :—" Well, Cousin, if you really mean to go I can only say I am sorry, and you must come back when you can. Give Sue my love and tell her I hope you and she may be happy."

HOFIUS :—" You do? well, so do I; but I've seen girls that I liked just as well as I do her, and they haint very far from me this minnit, neither; I could reach one of them; but Sue is good enough, I spose, I shall go right home and marry her, too; so good bye, Mabel." [*Shakes hand, puts arm around and kisses her while using handkerchief.*]

MABEL :—" Hof., don't feel so bad: I shall go down and see you when you are married and happy."   [Both exit L.]

NORA :—[*Entering.*] " Now, sure, what good thing comes nixt? I niver see the loikes of that feller, an' he's gone. Ah, Nora McCarty, ye feel relaved. (*Dusting.*) twinty toimes has he scart the brith from me body; but he is a little the resimblince of me own poor Tim, somethin' loike a singed cat, better'n he looks. Tim niver see the crazy spells loike him. Yis, he's gone, and good riddance. Now I'll read me letther agin. (*Takes letter from pocket. Thinking.*) 'Pon me soul. I forgit the commincemint! Mabel was crazy a gitin' on her foine fixins for the party, an' she read it too fast. Let me see. Ah, yis, I have it now. (*Reads.*) 'Me darlint Nora, darlint Nora.' That's Tim. 'Nora, darlint, I may niver behold those beautiful eyes any more, and thin, agin. I may. I am goin' to beautiful America.' He will have to stop that drinkin' if he comes here. (*Raises voice.*) 'Darlint Nora,' " [*Enter Hofius for book. Nora tries to conceal letter. Frightened.*]

HOFIUS :—" I forgot my book. Nora. (*Gets book.*) Got another letter from your mither, Nora darlint? "

NORA :—" No, sir; there's no letther here; an' it's none o' yer business, if ye plaze, sir, if I have."

HOFIUS :—" Your mother must have been a great writer to stick to you so long after she is dead. But then, John Brown kept marching on years after he was dead. Good bye, Nora." (*She turns her back and he yells good bye last. Nora frightened. Exit L.*]

NORA:—" Farewell, and may ye niver come back." [*Enter Hilton*]

HILTON:—" Where is Minnie? I thought I heard her in **here**. Perhaps she is bidding Hof. good bye. Well, I am glad he has gone, his presence has not always been entirely agreeable." [*Exit Nora. Enter Minnie.*]

MINNIE·—" Here I am, Uncle. (*Climbs into Hilton's lap, shows flowers.*) Look at these flowers, are they not pretty? They were sent to Mabel and Gertie for the party. How fragrant!"

HILTON:—" Yes they are beautiful. Where are the girls?" ·

MINNIE:—" Dressing for the party. When I get to be a young lady can I go to the parties with them?"

HILTON:—" Certainly, my dear; but I am glad you are young, as I now have your company at home."

MINNIE:—" Perhaps I ought to take these flowers to them."

HILTON:—" No, sit still; they will come for them when needed. I did not know you were so fond of flowers."

MINNIE:—" I am very fond of flowers, let me put these on the table. (*Puts them on table.*) When I was a little mite of a girl and lived at my Papa's home, Mamma had such beautiful flowers. Oh, Uncle! you never saw my Mamma; she was so good, so pretty and she loved me so." [*Sobs.*]

HILTON:—" I know your Mamma must have loved you; Mabel and I love you, we could not live without you, Minnie." [*Minnie's arms encircle his neck.*]

MINNIE: –" I am so glad: I think so much of you all; but sometimes I dream of Mamma and Papa; they looked so natural, so sweet to me. I'll never see them 'til I die, will I, Uncle?" [*Sobs.*]

HILTON:—" No, darling. I have often wondered, Minnie, why you call me Uncle; your father gave you to me and you are my daughter."

MINNIE:—" I will tell you: Papa's brother, who visited us when we were at home, was so nice and good that you made me think of him. He died the same summer Mamma did. I call you Uncle because you are so good to me. I cannot call you Papa. (*Sobs.*) I remember my dear Papa so well, he suffered so much for me; I love you, Uncle, but I cannot call you Papa."

HILTON: –" I would not ask it if you did not prefer it."

MINNIE:—" Don't you remember, Uncle, when he said he was glad to die, that he would no longer be in my way, and that I could have a good home? (*Sobs and cries.*) I cannot forget his face, so sweet and pale as he lay there dying, (*Crying.*) going home to Mamma. No, no; I can never call another Papa."

HILTON:—" Hush, darling; I would not have my little girl do anything that would be painful to her."

MINNIE:—" You never saw my Papa when he was well and strong; he was a grand looking man. No, you never saw he and Mamma; they dressed so prettily; we had such a nice home, beautiful flowers, pretty birds; I had little dolls and play houses, and Mamma would sing to me; everybody loved Papa and Mamma, everybody. I wish you could hear them sing. Mamma used to sing me songs about the angels; I wish I could have gone with them and been an angel, too. But I couldn't die, we can't die when we want to, can we, Uncle?"

HILTON:—" Why, Minnie, had you gone with your Papa I would have been alone. Mabel loves me, but she is no longer a little girl like you. I am glad you are here to be my little angel; to sit on my lap and kiss me." [*Enter Gertie R.*]

GERTIE:—" Oh, Uncle, what would we do without Minnie? what would you do without her? How often I wish myself a little girl, too; so happy, no cares, light hearted and free. Oh, what would I give to blot out all and place myself back to childhood. I feel that this life is scarcely worth living for; so many regrets! this life is full of regrets; it is wrong to say it, I suppose, yet we cannot always remain silent and suffer."

MINNIE:—" Cousin Gertie, I feel just as bad as you do, sometimes. If I were a young lady and could go to parties and dress like you and Mabel, look as you do when dressed for parties, and be so beautiful, *I* would be happy always. (*Caressing Hilton.*) But Uncle is so kind to me I must not say such things; I love to be with him and sit on his lap."

GERTIE:—" Ah, Minnie, parties, dress and dancing are only outside show; no genuine happiness comes from society. But you are too young to talk of sorrows." [*Minnie gets down and gets flowers for Gertie.*]

MINNIE:—" Here are the flowers, arn't they pretty? they will look pretty with that lovely dress. You are beautiful, Gertie." [*Kisses her.*]

GERTIE:—" Thank you, Darling." [Minnie exit L.]

HILTON:—" I agree with Minnie; you certainly look charming, Gertie."

GERTIE:—" Thank you, Uncle; I acknowledge feeling flattered when you compliment me."

HILTON:—" So you think your Uncle's judgment worth something, do you? well now I feel flattered. I was afraid you would never forgive the past, that you would never consent to live again in my home; I am glad you can overlook it. I was badly deceived, Gertie."

GERTIE:—" Uncle, I never blamed you entirely. I knew you were being deceived; I, too, have been deceived; how I have suffered God alone knows, yet I am thankful that I can remember the time when my heart was as light as June's brightest day, or the bee, the bird, the butterfly when on their lightest wing; but ah, those sunny days! the clouds have passed over them, and I have suffered, I have been wronged shamefully. I have prayed that something might come to take me from this world, from so much false show; but I lived on until now I am hardened. I love you and Mabel dearly as ever, but other people, other things no longer effect me. I am truly thankful." [*Enter Mabel dressed for party.*]

MABEL:—" Gertie, we are late, I fear. What pretty flowers! We must put on our wraps." [*Exit Mabel and Gertie L.*]

HILTON:—" Why, where is Minnie? I did not miss her until now." [*Exit, taking paper.*]

SCENE II. *Moonlight-Path.*

LOCENO:—[*Creeping through.*] " Ah, these old woods look natural; this path and the little grove beyond. How many times I have sang my songs here with Gertie. What if they should see me and know me! No, they shall not. How happy I might have been! Oh, Gertrude Mason, I hope you will know what it is to love and loose that love. Have I deserved so much? I would have been kind to Gertie. Mabel Hilton, curse you! you, too, shall suffer. Your lover is a jealous one. What can I do? Harry Hanford, Mabel, Gertie and all; I must have revenge! This life of mine is worth little. I will see Harry Hanford this night." [Exit L.]

SCENE III.

House in the distance—Lawn—Rustic seats—Moonlight—Music and dancing heard—Ernest and Gertie come down arm in arm.

ERNEST:—" Miss Gertie, that waltz was charming. You seem to enjoy dancing more than in olden times, or when I first knew you."

GERTIE:—" Yes, my tastes are somewhat different. Perhaps you may remember telling me that we change wonderfully in ideas as we grow older. I have not realized the change only as I compare my thoughts of eighteen with those of twenty-three; how different I am; how different I feel. I have often wished to be back to the unsophisticated age, when I believed in everything and everybody."

ERNEST: --" Ah, Miss Mason, do you mean what you say? You certainly cannot be indifferent to all the admiration that is bestowed upon you. I valued your society when I first knew you, but now I return to find you even more charming. My dear Gertie, you cannot term this flattery; you certainly must feel your worth; all society is ready to drop on bended knee to you."

GERTIE:—" You must remember that my wealth makes admirers; say it is, Ernest, as it is so uninteresting to talk of one's self. (*Looks at left frightened.*) Ernest, who is that crawling through the trees? can you see?" [*Pointing to left.*]

ERNEST:—" I can see but not very distinctly."•

GERTIE:—" If I thought it could be I would say it was Loceno Diuppa, it looks so like him. (*Shudders.*) Oh, I shudder to think of him! 'Tis very foolish to mention him as it cannot be. (*Harry approaches.*) There is Harry, this is his waltz."

HARRY:—" This is my waltz, Gertie, and others are looking for you. Ernest should not be too selfish."

GERTIE:—" Are you not going to return with us?" [*Go toward house. Ernest remains.*]

ERNEST:—" No, thanks; I enjoy the moonlight, but will be there in time for my dance. I assure you. (*Exit Harry and Mabel.*) I do not doubt there being several waiting for her. Why did I not seize the prize three years ago, when I could? I loved her well enough then; I knew she idolized me. A man sometime, sooner or or later, suffers when he casts aside a loving heart; misery is bound to come to him sometime. 'Twas cruel to treat her so; she who was so worthy, so loving, would have died to save me. I was thoughtless, I did not realize what I was doing. She prefers my society to others, but I fear she is too high-spirited to forget and come to me now. She was lovely at twenty but oh, how gloriously beautiful at twenty-three. Never before have I felt inferior when in a lady's society; I have always felt the assurance that I had only to woo and I could win; but now with her it seems improbable. (*Rises to go.*) Happy when near her, miserable when away. (*Ernest meets Harry, Mabel and Gertie.*) I was going to claim the number on my program; I see you are getting selfish, too."

HARRY:—" No, I am not; you can have them both."

MABEL:—" Shall I return with them, Harry? "

HARRY:—" No, come with me. (*Exit Gertie and Ernest. Harry and Mabel come down front and sit on rustic seat.*) Mabel, I have something to say to you that pains me more than you can ever know; something that I would never have dreamed you guilty of. It came from the lips of a stranger to me as he was talking to another person. I heard your name and I listened; 'twas while you were dancing with that Frank Smith. I acknowledge I have often accused you wrongfully, but I cannot be mistaken this time. (*He looks at her sternly.*) You are very silent; you think it useless to talk."

MABEL:—" Yes, it is useless; you go on and finish as I haven't the least idea of what you intend saying."

HARRY:—" I have always thought that if your father would countenance that miserable Frank Smith you would marry him; I have heard enough to-night to convince me, and now I see why you act so strangely. You love him instead of me; you have worshipped him from childhood, and you accept my company that you may meet him. He has boasted to others that I would soon know just where I belonged; that you were reared in elegance, and that marrying a poor lawyer was something you never dreamed of. Mabel, you should be woman enough to tell me."

MABEL:—[*Rising.*] " I am too much of a woman to act that which I do not feel. So many times have I heard something similar to this, and so many times I have asked forgiveness when there was no reason for me to ask to be forgiven, yet I have humored you in this unreasonable jealousy. You should be man enough to know, to appreciate, what I have endured for you. I have endured your fits of jealousy simply because you were not as wealthy as I. You ought to know me by this time; you should have more confidence in me than to credit such a story for a moment. It was a story gotten up expressly for your ears, and to hurt your feelings; an enemy of yours or mine, perhaps. You know how dearly I love you, but I cannot always ask forgiveness for something I am perfectly ignorant of. Not a word of that which you have repeated is true. I can no longer endure this, Harry; if this is a specimen of what my life is to be, to be ever in fear of your jealousy, why, it will soon become a dread, and there will be no happiness for either. So, if you really believe this now—but sometime in the future you will realize your mistake; come to me, Harry, as I shall wait for you long as life lasts. I cannot ask forgiveness again when I am innocent of a wrong thought concerning you. (*Goes toward house.*) Good bye."

HARRY:—[*Surprised.*] "I am surprised; she has always been so meek before. I never thought Mabel could talk like that; she would ask forgiveness when I was all to blame; but I am not to blame now; this man knew her well; she has loved Frank Smith from childhood. I know she gives him the nicest dances on the program, and, again, it may be an enemy. Yet, he told the story so plain, drew the picture so real! I could never wed a woman who loved another. Yes, I believe his story and yet, how dare I dispute Mabel? " [*Goes toward house.*]

SCENE IV.

Same as in SCENE II—Enter Loceno, smiling.

LOCENO:—"Ah ha! I knew his jealous nature! He will never know me and a doubt will always cling to him. She will suffer a little if. not the most intense. He is a jealous man. and sometime in the future, when she thinks she is happy, he will relate this story I told him to-night. He will not forget it. for, mark me, a jealous man never forgets. (*Takes out paper.*) Now I will write to Mrs. Howard; she is in the far West, and any news concerning the unhappiness of Mabel will be thankfully received. (*Writes.*) ' My dear Mrs. Howard: I saw Harry Hanford—'. I am weaker to-day than usual. (*Silence, as if writing. Puts letter in pocket.*) Now, when she reads this she will know why I am so far away. I saw Gertie in the mazy dance; Gertie, beautiful as ever! and she saw me, yet she could not believe it was Loceno, but the strong resemblance made her shudder; a shudder! I could die happy could she smile on me once; no smile, but instead—a shudder! There is nothing for me here. There is a little rock on the river edge, not far from here; one leap and 't will all be over. No I was not a fit companion for human being, but I can be food for the fish. (*Goes toward wood.*) Food for the fish! " [*Takes out handkerchief to wipe face and letter falls unnoticed. Exit.*]

SCENE V.

Frame house—Yard—Walk from Left—Sign overdoor, "SUE WRIGHT, MILLINER & DRESS-MAKER."—Several couple go in—Lantern hangs at door. —Hofius walking toward house with violin.

HOFIUS:—" Now, darned if I don't think Squash Holler is improvin' fast. Milliner shop, blacksmith shop; well I'll give 'em some new jigs to-night. (*Reads sign.*) 'Sue Wright, Milliner and Dressmaker.' I wish Gertie and Mabel were here to-night, they'd see a *dance* if I do manage the bow. Guess I'll play a little and see if they air expecting me." [*Sits under window playing when Sue comes to door. Sue lisps.*]

SUE:—" Hof. Hathkins, come right in here; why did you come tho late? I geth it ith thum of your new-fangled ideaths you got up at your Uncle Jim's. Out of thith, we are all ready to danth." [*Steps out by him.*]

HOFIUS:—" Golly, Sue, you are right up in all the fashion."

SUE:—" Do you thuppose becauth we live in the country that we don't know what sthyle is? we do, you bet."

HOFIUS:--" Don't talk so tarnel hateful. Susie; you know I like you, don't you."

SUE:—" I alwayth thuppposed you did."

HOFIUS:--" No suppose to it, I always did. I can play some new waltzes. (*Plays, leans toward her.*) My hand goes pretty fast, don't it? (*Kisses her. She wipes mouth with sleeve. Hof. Laughs.*) You see; Susie, that's where the extra comes in. don't you? "

SUE:—" Thaths real mean in you. (*Laughs.*) I can't help laughin' but I am mad."

HOFIUS:—" Now, Susie, don't get cantankerous when you know I like you, don't you, Susie? "

SUE:—" I alwayths thuppposed you did,"

HOFIUS:—" Now, before we go in, tell me what your favorite is."

SUE:—" The girl I left behind me; the way you used to call it, so it would come in rhyme and sounded so pretty."

HOFIUS:—" All right; I always do as you want me to, don't I, Sue? "

SUE:—" I alwayths thuppposed you did."

They go in—Two more couple come up walk, knock and enter —Loud laughing —Tuning violin, heard within—House parts finding Hofius playing the violin, 'Girl I left behind me,' beating time with foot.

SCENE VI.   *Kitchen—Interior.*

HOFIUS:--" All take pardners an' form on for 'Girl I left behind me.' (*A number crowd on, Sue and her partner ahead.*) No crowdin' around there. Hello there, Bill snooks, you and Sam Wilson wait 'till next dance. (*They retire unwillingly.*) Are you all ready fur biz? (*All reply Yes.*) If I wasn't the fiddler Susie knows who I would dance with, don't you, Sue? "

SUE:—" I alwayth thupposed I did." [*Orchestra plays ' Girl I left behind me.*')

HOFIUS: --" *Address* your sweetness.

    First two couple forward and back ;
    Sides two couple, mind you,
    Balance to your *lady* fair
    And *swing* that girl behind you.

(*Plays last half over.*)

    Oh. balance to yer pardner agin,
    Then to the right she passes,
    Oh, ladies, swing the right-hand gent,
    Then swing yer honey molasses.
    Oh. gir-rils swing the right-hand gent,
    Then swing yer honey molasses,
    First gent balance to the lady at the right,
     Then swing his little rosa,
    All jine hands hands and circle to the left,
    Then swing each little posie.
    Oh forward all and back agin,
    And listen to the fiddle,
    Boys, swing your lasses half-way 'round
    And crack ' er down in the middle.
    Boys, swing yer duckies half-way 'round
    And crack ' er down in the middle.

(*Draws bow over strings.*) Seats! (*Exit through side door, crowd each other in going out. Hofius wipes forehead.*) I tell you that's *dancing*; makes the sweat run.   It's biz to play for a dance. Guess I'll git a drink of cider." [*Exit through door. Scene closes in.*]

SCENE VII.

Path as in SCENE II—Enter Gertie and Mabel dressed for a walk.

GERTIE:—" How strange you talk, Mabel."

MABEL:—" Really, Gertie, I am almost sorry I said it."

GERTIE:—" Mabel, do you repent so soon? What did you say to Harry that sounds so terrible? "

MABEL:—"Oh, I said—I do not know as I remember exactly; but one thing was this: that if I ever spoke to him again it would be when he came to me. Perhaps I said worse things; I hope not; perhaps I did, but I hope not, I hope I did not! "

GERTIE:—" Mabel, so long as you humor him in his jealousy, just so long he will have those spells; perhaps he will until you belong to him."

MABEL:—" Our wedding day was near at hand, yet he remains away."

GERTIE:—" I will tell you what to do."

MABEL:—" Do not tell me anything wrong, for Harry isn't so very bad after all."

GERTIE:—" Why dear Mabel, do you think I would have you do Harry a wrong? Do you remember when you told me what course to pursue in regard to Ernest? Am I not being repaid? I took your advice and to-day I see him worshipping me as I did him, and I glory in it. He turned from me once as though I was a little child, or as though a broken heart was soon mended; but soon he will know how to sympathize with the broken-hearted. To-morrow he wishes to see me alone; how I have worked for this; how untiring have been my efforts; and to-morrow he shall be paid! He thinks I love him, and when he asks for my love, ah, Mabel, I shall see him suffer as I have suffered. But how selfish to talk of my affairs and neglect yours."

MABEL:—" I like to listen to you, but Harry has not done so bad as Ernest; I could not take such advice as that."

GERTIE:—" I can say nothing against Harry, only let him go awhile, he will soon see his mistake and humbly ask forgiveness."

MABEL:—" Then I wish he would hurry, I cannot wait much longer. How could he believe such a falsehood! This is not the first time he has been angry, and I was angry, and ugly, too. Harry is so sweet I cannot imagine why he should ever be hateful; he may never forget."

GERTIE:—" I believe you are fretting unnecessarily."

MABEL:—" Perhaps I am, but I am terribly in love! (*Gertie laughs.*) I am, truly. I feel cross toward everyone; I want to scold and fret continually; but one word from Harry would bring me out as tame and docile. (*Exit Gertie L.*) Oh, dear! oh, dear! Yes, 'tis true; if Harry says the meanest things imaginable to me, he has only to turn around and say: ' Come here, little kitten,' and I come, mewing and purring along to him; if the next moment he says scat, I scat. (*Looks for Gertie.*) Am I alone? I presume I ought to be, and Gertie has probably gone away disgusted. Some people can be in love and retain their senses, but as Cousin Hofius would say, 'taint me, (*Leaving.*) 'taint me." [*Exit L. Enter Ernest and Gertie.*]

ERNEST:—" I am glad I met you; how did you happen here alone? Where is Mabel? "

GERTIE:—" I left her here; she was feeling rather down-hearted. Everyone has their sorrows."

ERNEST: —" You cannot have any sorrows; you have all that is required to make one happy. To make one happy, if you are not, I would like to know is required."

GERTIE:—" Would you? sometime I may tell you."

ERNEST:—" You may tell me to-morrow when I call. You will be there, will you not? "

GERTIE:—" Certainly. I shall be here and anxiously awaiting your coming." [*Ernest tips hat and exit L. Gertie bows and exit R.*]

SCENE VIII.

Parlor as in SCENE 1—Nora enters flourishing letter.

NORA:—" I wonder, I wonder where is Miss Mabel? The girral is niver here whin I calls her; an' a letther, too, for her; aint it a big letther? may be it's from her swate-heart. Spakin' o' swate-hearts makes me think o' Tim, poor, long-forgotten Tim. In his last letther he writes he expects to be here soon. Ah, Tim, your Nora is waitin' an' watchin' fur yez, watchin' an' waitin', waitin' an' watchin'. Ah, heaven bless me. (*Enter Mabel.*) Here's a letther, Miss Mabel." [*Mabel throws herself despondently in a chair.*]

MABEL:—" Take my hat and wraps; I am too tired to read anyone's letter, put it on the table. [*Nora puts it on table.*]

NORA:—" Sure, an' it's not me that could rest aisy a knowin' that such a big, fat letther was waitin' me to read. No, no; not Nora McCarty." [Exit L.]

MABEL:—" I wonder why Gertie does not come. I am so tired."
[*Enter Hilton and Minnie holding hands. Minnie carries book.*]

MINNIE·—" I have read the book you gave me, Mabel; see what a lovely one Uncle gave me this morning; isn't it pretty? Uncle, tell Mabel what we are *all* going to do."

HILTON:—" I am going to Drury Lake on business in a few days and thought it would be pleasant for you, Minnie and Gertie to accompany me." [*Enter Gertie.*]

MINNIE:—[*Delighted.*] " You came too late to hear the news; we are all going to Drury Lake on a pleasure excursion; and (*Shows book.*) look at my beautiful new book."

GERTIE:—" It is a lovely book. Where did you say we were going? "

HILTON:—" Ernest and I are obliged to go to Drury Lake on important business and thought it would be a pleasant trip for all."

GERTIE:—" I am willing, am sure I would enjoy it; and you, too, are going, are you, Minnie? "

MINNIE:—" Yes, we are *all* going. (*Mabel rises and opens letter.*) Come into the library, Uncle, please." [Both exit.]

MABEL:—[*Showing delight and surprise.*] " Oh, Gertie! you cannot tell who it is from, and such a long one, too."

GERTIE:—" I will warrant it is from penitent Harry; your face tells me as much."

MABEL:—" Yes, yes; listen: 'Darling Mabel!' Ha, ha! 'You little abused darling; I feel so guilty, so ashamed of myself' That sounds just like Harry. 'To think that I should accuse you of deceiving me; there was not a word of truth in it.' I told Harry there was no truth in it. 'The story was told by Loceno Diluppa and intended for my ears. He lost the letter he wrote and I found it.' "

GERTIE:—" Loceno Diluppa! there, I knew I saw him the night of the party; I knew his wicked (*Shudders.*) face."

MABEL: —" ' The letter was written to Mrs. Howard; I found it near the Deep River valley, where he put an end to his life.' There, Gertie, he will frighten us no more. 'Darling Mabel, I have caused you many tears.' I should think he had. (*Sobs.*) I always cry when Harry and I have a fuss; I must cry. Oh, dear! isn't this a good letter? 'I am anxious to see you, and, dear Mabel, forgive me this

once; I shall never be so silly again.' He knows I will forgive him.
He signs his name in the same peculiar style; look! " [*Shows letter,
Gertie laughs.*]

GERTIE:—" Why, Mabel, the letter is turned wrong side up."

MABEL:—[*Laughing.*] It is? It is Harry, anyway. Gertie, I am
just as happy as I can be. I am so glad he found out the truth of
the matter. I must write him immediately, shall I not, Gertie? "

GERTIE:—" Certainly; Harry is penitent, acknowledges his wrongs
and, in fact, a splendid fellow and loves you dearly, Mabel."

MABEL:—" I know he does, I know he loves me, but he is so
jealous."

GERTIE:—" And, if I am not mistaken, he is not altogether disagreeable to you."

MABEL:—" No, not entirely so; but I believe I will tease him a
while; he knows how silly I am and he is confidant he will get an
answer this very day, and I guess I will wait 'till to-morrow. (*Looks
at letter.*) Yet, it is a sweet little letter, and supposing something
would happen him soon and I have it on my mind that he was neg-
lected a moment; perhaps I had better write; I will do just as you
say."

GERTIE:—" You should write, as there will be no rest for you, he
or any of us so long as you are waiting."

MABEL:—" I like your advice, but cannot say as much for the
manner you have of expressing yourself. Where were you so long
this afternoon? "

GERTIE:—" I met Ernest unexpectedly; he was, as usual, pleased
to meet me; spoke again of his wishing to see me alone. The
time is near, Mabel; I long for revenge, and yet, I shall miss the
pleasant morning calls, the afternoon visits, the evenings at the
opera where the music had found a charm it had not possessed in
years. All the hours and days that glide so goldenly into our hopes
and dreams that they become henceforth so inseperable that in no
sense of retrospection are we able to tell whether the sunshine
made the vision so beautiful, or the dream lit the hours with untold
glory. Ah, yes; I shall miss it all; cast it aside for revenge; yet,
why am I to pray for revenge, when every christian teaches forgiveness to our foes? "

MABEL:—" It does seem wicked when you know he loves you;
but you say you cannot forgive him."

GERTIE:—" I could but I do not care to; no, I shall not act the
baby now. He has seen me excel in all my undertakings; he saw

me try to conceal the tears the day he left me in the little park; he had no pity for me then and I have none for him to-day. If there are any tears shed he shall shed them." [*Enter Nora.*]

NORA:—" Mr. Vaughn wishes to see Miss Gertrude."

GERTIE:—" Oh, tell him I await his presence in the parlor." [*Exit Nora.*]

MABEL:—" Gertie, I feel very sorry for you, sorry for Ernest. Perhaps you are doing injustice to yourself."

GERTIE:—" I think not; you go and write to Harry."

MABEL:—" Yes, I shall as soon as I get to my room." [*Exit Mabel. Enter Ernest.*]

ERNEST:—" Good evening, Gertrude. [*Leads her to sofa.*] I am pleased to see you looking so happy. I sincerely hope what I may say to you will not change the expression of your face."

GERTIE:—" If my face expresses happiness then, indeed, it speaks the language of my heart."

ERNEST:—" You undoubtedly know why I asked to see you alone. Gertrude, I love you; love you with all the strength of my manhood, all the power of my soul. You may think it strange that I could wait no longer; but, Gertie, could you but realize the great depth of my affection you would pardon all. I know that I should have waited 'till I earned it, only forgive me that I could not. I ask only half the affection I give you. Can you ever care for me? (*Remains silent.*) Are you angry, Gertie, that you do not answer me?"

GERTIE:—" No, no; I am not angry."

ERNEST:—" Then do not longer punish me. You must care something for me. God could not be so unkind, so cruel as to send this great love to me only to be a blight on my life. Can you love me? Did you ever care for me?"

GERTIE:—" Did I ever care for you? Ah, Ernest, that is an idle question. You know how much I loved you. Did I love you? oh, heavens! better than the whole world; than my own life. if I had not loved you would I have asked you to picture the woman to me that you could call 'wife,' and I not spare any pains to make myself as near the picture as I could so that you would love me as dearly as I did you?"

ERNEST:—[*Kneeling, kisses hand.*] " Do you mean what you tell me? Gertrude, did you do this that I might some day love you?"

GERTIE:—" Yes; let me tell you: I was younger when I first met you; I knew nothing of the selfishness of this world; I met you, I thought you loved me; you gave me every reason to think it; you grew to be my idol; I worshipped every move; your actions told me your love, until the last moment when you left me. I struggled to conceal the tears, but you saw them, Ernest."

ERNEST:—" Gertrude, my great love can only repay you. Gertrude, do you love me now as you did then? "

GERTIE:—" Do I? Here is the little flower you gave me the day you left me in the park; I have kept it as a memento of the sweetest days of my life and the bitterest. You say you love me, Ernest; do you love me, Ernest, love me dearly as I did you? "

ERNEST:—" I have said to you what I never said to woman before; I come to you with the question from my soul to yours, finding in you the womanly nature for which my heart has yearned. You are my idol, perfect as God could make it."

GERTIE:—" You may think differently. You love me! How I have longed to hear you say this. I have labored to win this from you, and I have succeeded beyond my expectations. (*Rises*,) But, Ernest Vaughn, why did I want you to love me? for revenge! " [*He rises and stares.*]

ERNEST:—" What? what? "

GERTIE:—" I have longed to hear you say that you loved me; I know you do with your whole soul, and I glory in it! "

ERNEST:—" Are you mad, or are you a demon? "

GERTIE:—" Neither, neither; but I remember three years ago when you left me so mercilessly, and the memory of that baffled affection has rendered my life miserable. (*Ernest weeps.*) Oh, weep; tears befit those eyes that send grief into their beams; those shining eyes, which, like the serpent, have charmed only to kill." [*Ernest falls on knees, spreads handkerchief over face.*]

ERNEST:—" Mercy! mercy! Oh, heaven, have mercy! "

GERTIE:—" Did you have mercy when you taught me to love you so much that only death could have seperated me from you until you scorned my love and turned it to hatred? I know that you love me, that you will always love me; your life will be one living curse to you as mine has been to me."

ERNEST:—" Forbear, forbear; my heart is breaking. Oh, Gertrude, God knows I did not realize what I done. Oh, I could forgive anything in you. You never loved me or you would not be so merciless." [*Rises.*]

GERTIE:—" I loved you wildly, passionately, but it was a trifling matter with you."

ERNEST:—" But, Gertrude—"

GERTIE:—" I will not listen, I cannot; my faith is gone, my hope is gone. You have taught me to be so wicked I cannot forgive you."

ERNEST:—" If I have been false, you have been none the less so. (*Retreats slowly.*) God forgive us! Do I deserve so much? Forgive me! " [Exit.]

GERTIE:—" He's gone, gone; and I have had my revenge. I have lived for revenge, yes, suffered, but revenge is at last mine! Yet, 'tis a cowardly thing to do. No heart? Ah, Ernest Vaughn, you can never dream of one truth, the love that filled my heart; and to-day I have cast it aside! He says if he has been false I have been none the less so. True, too true! He did not make it the study of years to make me suffer. How plainly I see those pleading eyes begging for mercy, and I laughed at his pleading. No, no; I am the wicked one. Oh, what torture! I feel a queer sensation, one that the guilty feel. But he has gone, gone! If he has been false I have been none the less so! No forgiveness, he has gone. Too late, too late; he has gone and I have sent him. The winds ring out the funeral knell of departed hopes and vanished resolutions. My life is a lonely one; but when with him the earth is beautiful, life then is worth living for. Could we forget and forgive? Could I be happy with him now if he could forgive? Could I? Is there no one to tell me, no one to advise me? No, no; no one; I am alone. (*Kneels in attitude of prayer.*) Merciful Father, hear and forgive." [*Scene closes in while she remains in prayer.*]

SCENE IX.

Path as in SCENE VII.—Enter Ernest slowly.

ERNEST:—" I wonder why Harry does not come, I have waited long and anxiously. I will walk along, perhaps I may meet him. What shall I say to him? Oh, Gertrude! that name, the one absolving thought of my nature; must I live without you, live only to think of the gem I have lost? No, she will never forgive! If she was at my mercy, oh, how gladly would I clasp her to my heart and forgive; but women do not forgive as easily as men. Perhaps I shall see her again, but my courage has gone. Merciful Heaven, sustain me!" [*Exit L. Enter Tim Finnegan drawing paper from pocket.*]

TIM:—" Nora, me darlint, you would niver suspect seein' yer Tim: but he's here, Nora, an' full o' Oirish thricks. Ah, Nora, I will decave ye (*puts on whiskers.*) wid these whiskers. But where is the letther she last wrote me? Here it is; the last letther. Ah, me little darlint, she'll go wild wid joy whin she sets her two beautiful eyes on her darlint Tim. (*Reads.*) ' Me own swate-heart, Tim; I am nearly wild wid grief a livin' an' a livin' here alone an' alone all me days, and you a livin' in ould Oireland.' Ah, he, he! she's badly decaved for I am here; Tim's here. Begorra, Nora, an' I'll rade more of the swate letther: ' Ah, Tim, I think of ye all the long day, an' niver a bit o' slape comes to me eyes for the dramin' o' yiz, Don't I moind the hat, the green band, that beautiful necktie and that illegant rid hair with the beautiful mouth and the beautiful face. Ah, Tim, I wud know yez among a hundred that looked jist loike ye. Come to America, Tim, me boy; I love ye an' am true to me swate-heart.' (*Puts letter in pocket.*) Why, Nora, I niver doubted yer love. (*Goes off stage slowly. Singing.*) Don't think that iver I'll doubt ye; me love I'll niver conceal."   [Exit.]

SCENE X.

Grove and flowers—Hilton holding Minnie's head among the blossoms.

HILTON:—" What is that flower, do you know its name? " [*Enter Harry and Mabel.*]

MINNIE:—" Some kind of a pink. Here's Mabel and Harry. Oh, Mabel, to-morrow we go to Drury Lake; I am so glad, arn't you, Mabel? We may stay a whole week, perhaps longer."

HARRY:—" I did not know you were anticipating a visit."

MABEL:—" I thought of going with Papa, Ernest, Gertie and Minnie."

HARRY:—" So I was to be left out; you wouldn't leave me now, would you? "

MABEL:—" No, certainly; I would not go now unless you could." [*Harry laughs.*]

HARRY:—" You are a courageous little armful." [*Hilton turns and laughs.*]

HILTON:—" Such performances are better appreciated when the parties are alone, I should think." [*Mabel and Harry look silly.*]

HARRY:—" Excuse me; I had forgotten anyone was near; I will try to be more circumspect in the future. Mr. Hilton, will you accompany me to the office? I have the papers for Minnie's money all straight now. I would like to have Minnie and Mabel go to the office, too, if they will."

HILTON:—" Certainly we will go; come girls." [*All exit L. Enter Gertie R.*]

NORA:—[*Enter back.*] " Miss Gertrude, did you see Mr. Hilton? A gintleman wants to spake wid him. It is the Mr. Vaughn; he looks so sorraful I belave he must be goin' away."

GERTIE:—" Then Uncle was the only person he asked to see? "

NORA:—" Yis; (*Enter Tim L.*) he said: 'Do you know, Nora, if Mr. Hilton is in?' an' I says: 'I'll go an' see.' " [*Gertie sits in front.*]

TIM:—" Plaze, ma'm, kin you tell me how long the distance is from here to Mr. Hilton's risidence? " [*Nora points at house.*]

NORA:—" Yis. sur; right there is the house, and this is their grove, but he isn't in there, or he wasn't whin I left the house, but he may be there this very minit."

TIM:—" Thin ye air acquainted in the family, air ye? "

NORA:—" Aint I though? Don't I work there week afther week, month afther month, day afther day? "

TIM:—" Listen, thin, an' I'll tell ye: There is a gintleman in the ould counthry that loves their maid, Nora; an' he said I must come here an' tell her so mesilf; an' that he will soon come to America."

NORA:—" Heavens an' mercy! Holy mither! do ye mean Tim? An' did ye behold Tim's beautiful face wid yer own eyes? "

TIM:—" Ah ha, yis. Does she remimber her ould swate-heart, Tim? "

NORA:—" She thinks o' Tim ivery day. Ah, yis; I know the girrul well, an' it's dyin' she is to look on his swate face; an' she will die of a broken heart if I can't see him." [*Puts apron to eyes while Tim takes off whiskers and goes to her.*]

TIM: -" Nora, me darlint, this is yer own beautiful Tim."

NORA;--[*Screaming.*] " Ah, Lord be praised! Why did ye decave me? Oh, heaven bless ye! Oh, Holy Mother, I shall die! " [*Faints and falls; Tim and Gertie rub her hands.*]

TIM:—" Ah. Nora, is it dyin' ye air? Me long lost Nora, air ye dead? Oh, me darlint, spake to me once and tell me air ye dead. Shmile on yer own beautiful Tim, and don't kape so soilent; shmile wid that beautiful mouth once more. Say, Nora, air ye dyin'? (*Rises and runs in all directions.*) Let me git some wather; where shall I go? "

NORA:—" Tim, no use to go fur wather, as it's dead I am by this toime. (*Enter Ernest and Minnie L. Nora rises, acts angry.*) Say, Tim, they air all comin' here, no toime fur me to git through wid the faintin'. Pick up yer wig an' we'll go to the house. (*Tim laughs loud.*] Tim, don't laugh so loud, ye'll kill me, for me head is nearly split open wid pain." [*Takes Tim's arm, throws roll of clothes over back, exit back.*]

MOONLIGHT.

Gertie confused and Ernest sad—Minnie laughing at Tim.

ERNEST;—" Good evening, Gertrude; it seems that you have been witnessing quite a scene."

GERTIE:—" The sudden appearance of Nora's sweet-heart quite overcome her. Altogether, it was quite laughable."

MINNIE:—" Doesn't he look funny? Cousin Gertie, you hate to have Mr. Vaughn leave us, don't you?"

GERTIE:—" Certainly, Minnie; why do you ask?"

MINNIE:—" When I told him he must go and bid you good bye, he said you would not care to see him, but I knew you would, and you are glad he came, aren't you?"

GERTIE:—" Yes, Minnie, I am."

ERNEST:—" Children, in their innocence, wring falsehoods from the truthful, do they not, Gertie?"

GERTIE:—" Was it a falsehood?" [*Minnie interrupts.*]

MINNIE:—" I must go and meet Uncle; he is coming." [Exit L.]

ERNEST:—" How can it be true that you wanted to see me? If you hate me as you say, there can be no pleasure in seeing my face. Why am I so repulsive to you? when I love you with a love that absorbs my whole soul—my whole life. I have made a great mistake, and so have you. Does it look right for us to make each other miserable? I wish there was a way to retrieve the wrong, that you could forgive me; I could you, oh, so easily! No, you cannot forget. I shall go where I will never see your face again. I wish I might never look on face of woman again. Oh, Gertrude; you rejoice in my sufferings! If you have toiled for the purpose of seeing me suffer, you have not toiled in vain. Had you put a bullet through my heart, then I should have been out of my misery. I cannot remain here. (*Tim and Nora in the distance. Hilton and Minnie, Harry and Mabel, not noticing Ernest and Gertie.*) Oh, Gertrude; you do not even pity me! Have you no heart?"

GERTIE: —" I once had a heart." [*Ernest comes toward her.*]

ERNEST:--" Then are you heartless? Your face does not speak it. You will pardon me for coming to say farewell. The last time I shall ever look in your beautiful face! Yes, I must go! (*Clasps her in his arms and kisses passionately.*) Gertrude, can it be that I shall never see you again? Farewell! Gertie, farewell forever! (*Raises hand over head in supplication.*) Oh, God, forgive us, and, in your mercy, watch over her until we meet in heaven, where all things are forgiven! (*Staggers, puts hand on head.*) Farewell! " Ernest leaves slowly—Gertie tries to speak but cannot; at last she screams.

GERTIE:—" Ernest! He does not hear me. Ernest! (*Ernest re·turns, looks surprised.*) One moment: I know that I have been cruel, so cruel; I thought I was living for revenge, but oh, Ernest! I was living for your love; without it I shall die. Can you take me with all my faults? Can you forgive me? " [*He clasps her in his arms. All turn toward front.*]

ERNEST:—" With all my heart."

CURTAIN.

THE END.

www.ingramcontent.com/pod-product-compliance
Lightning Source LLC
Chambersburg PA
CBHW020042030726
47499CB00007B/2536